Banking On Love

Elia Fairburn

BAD CREATIVE BOOKS

This edition contains the complete text

of the original hardcover edition.

NOT ONE WORD HAS BEEN OMITTED.

BANKING ON LOVE

A Bad Creative Book / published by

arrangement with the author

Elia Faiburn

COVER DESIGN BY

Gestvlt

ISBN: 9781095838310

BAD CREATIVE PUBLISHING HISTORY

The Simplest Way To Learn French 2017

The Simplest Way To Learn Spanish 2017

Managing Complications In Anesthesia And Critical Care

Table Of Contents

CHAPTER 1

T's & C's

———— • ————

Tessa Clayton awoke to the sound of an obnoxious fog horn resounding from the speaker on her new iPhone, that sat atop the night stand beside her bed. She released a sluggish, pale, willowy arm from under the comforting cocoon she had made for herself from her duvet cover, to search in a limp, slapping motion for the offending source of the morning alarm. Finally, her long thin fingers made contact with the device's slim, silver body, and she pulled it under the covers with her to hit the snooze button. Her big beautiful green eyes, now somewhat scratchy and dry from being shut all night, squinted at the offensive glare of light coming from the screen of the mobile phone. A heavy, grumbling sigh escaped her parched lips, as she felt the cold of the room sweep over her bare legs and arms, after throwing off the mass of fabric that covered her. Tessa lay there for a moment more, staring at the stationary ceiling fan above her. Even though she loved being able to go to a job she enjoyed every day, she still had to catch her bearings. She had never really ever been much of a morning person, and the hours she was working for the financial firm required her to get up much earlier than she was accustomed.

Tessa swung the near dead weight of her tired legs over the side of the bed, and onto the cold of the imitation hardwood floor of her bedroom. The tendrils of cold tingled up through the bottoms of her bare feet, and up her legs, causing her to shiver and flinch as the little hairs stood up on the back of her neck. She knew it was only six thirty in the morning and she didn't have to be there until eight, but she needed to be up by this time. She needed to have the time to get ready, get her head on straight, and have had her full quota of caffeine, before facing the inevitable stampede that occurred every day on the street awaiting her outside.

Tessa got up and shuffled her way out of her small bedroom and into the even smaller kitchen of the studio apartment where she now dwelt. It made her think about how there were a lot of things that she was having to become accustomed to now that she lived here. Her life had most definitely undergone several changes since she moved in here with her now best friend, Shalena. Tessa had been so used to living in a more suburban area in upstate New York, in a three bedroom house, with a spacious kitchen and all the amenities with her boyfriend Tedd. Well, ex-boyfriend Tedd. Even though it had been a few months since their horrendous earth shattering break up, she still seemed to be hung up on him and the events that occurred between them; as Shalena liked to tell her practically every day. This is why she didn't make much of an effort to go to the bar where she worked on a regular basis, for she got enough of a lecture on how she so needed to move on with her life while she was at home.

As Tessa pulled down a green ceramic mug from the cabinet above the one-cup-serving coffee maker, she thought about how different she thought life would turn out while she was with Tedd. Everything had seemed so perfect leading up to her meeting him and even while they lived together. She was the typical girl next door, raised by somewhat upper middle class parents. The usual run of the mill blue collar family. Her mother was a nurse's assistant for the geriatric ward at the local memorial hospital. Her father, an engineer for a manufacturer of various car parts. Both parents worked very hard and long hours to provide for their children, and did their best to instill the same responsibility and work ethic into them as well. Though they never really had that much money to speak of, like so many of their neighbors and schoolmates, the Clayton's ensured that their children never wanted for anything. Especially, love and a good family support system. Tessa always figured this was due to the fact that both of her parents were only children, and had never really experienced what it was like to be a part of a tight family unit, like the one they so desperately tried to provide for her and her brother Geoffrey.

The Clayton's had settled down in the suburban area of upstate New York to get out of all the hustle and bustle of city life. They figured it was a better place to raise children than in the smog covered, overly populated, areas of the inner city. This way, they had access to what they felt were the best schools for their budget, and they didn't have to worry about their children being shot or worse while trying to learn. It was the perfect setting they felt, a little two story house with a lawn and a picket fence, with a quaint cove for the their kids to ride their bikes. Everything seemed ideal. Except for one simple detail, they didn't have any children. They had married a little later in life, both being the practical choosy sort of people that her parents are. So when they got together they were quite prepared to move out of the city, settle down, and start a family. When suddenly, and to their great horror, it was discovered that not only was her mother's womb considered inhospitable, but her father's swimmers were not exactly the most energetic. But somehow, by a miracle she guessed, they were eventually able to conceive her older brother Geoffrey. Her parents were overjoyed and showered him with all kinds of love and everything a little boy could ever ask for. This was mostly because they had also been told not to count on being able to conceive any other children after him, so they decided to pour all of the love that they had reserved for the many children they desired into him. Which was not such a bad idea, then something completely unexpected and equally miraculous occurred. They received the news, that even though they believed it was impossible for them to have more than one child, they were pregnant yet again with another. And, of course, this child was Tessa. Tessa felt that they were equally overjoyed at her arrival as they were for her brother's. Even though, sometimes she felt a bit overshadowed by him at times while they were growing up. There was never really any hard feelings or contentions between them because of his status as the eldest child, the miracle boy as they liked to title him still on occasions.

They both attended the same school, but attended different classes due to their differences in age and grades.

But this did not prevent them from spending a lot of time together as they grew up, or creating the same circle of friends. This group of friends included Kirsten and Tedd. The four of whom were as thick as thieves and seemingly inseparable from the time that they met in middle school. They even started their own sort of club with its own set of rules for people to join, and this led to many nights spent in tent forts with flashlights, in the living room of their parents' house, reading to each other. Both she and her brother had always had an affinity for learning. Though, their tastes were a bit different, as she had more of an inclination for all things practical and explicable by numbers, and he was more fascinated with art and world history. This is inevitably led them to pursuing separate majors in college. The four friends all attended the same college, and it seemed as if they would all spend the rest of their lives together, until that fateful day when all of their lives were utterly shattered and Tessa felt her world turn completely upside down.

The weekend was fast approaching. She and Geoffrey were about to make their customary journey to their parents' house for three days, to do laundry and eat regular food, as opposed to the fare they were usually exposed to on campus. But there was something different about this weekend, Tessa was already on her way to the house and Geoffrey was going to be coming after. They had spoken on the phone beforehand as Tessa departed the campus, and her brother had made her promise to call him when she arrived, to let him know she had made it safely, as was his usual practice. She, of course, acquiesced; even though she thought it was a bit silly and mother hen of him to think this way. Because, what could possibly happen? Nothing had ever happened before while they were on the way to visit their parents, so why would it start now? If nothing else, she thought that perhaps this was just his way of telling her that he loved her. Just another of his sweet gestures.

Tessa finally arrived at the family home, where she found her mother and father waiting for her as usual. They greeted her with the customary worrying and pecking of telling her that they couldn't wait until she and her brother had graduated, and could find a place to live closer to them, so things could go back to being the way they had always been. And, she would reassure them that everything was fine where they were and she didn't understand what they were so worried about. Also, that they would be graduated in another year or two, and that would be here before they even had time to blink. But what she didn't account for, was the fact that something else could occur that would threaten to derail all possibility of things ever being the same again. If not destroy the notion altogether.

She remembered the day as if it were yesterday, as she stood there in the lonely kitchen sipping on her freshly brewed piping hot black coffee. Tessa could see herself, having just changed into an oversized New York Giants jersey and her favorite pair of comfy sweat pants, with her long dark brown locks up in a mint green head band, and a gooey face mask to match all over her face. She made her way into the all too familiar living room of her parents' house and plopped down on the overstuffed beige couch, a few paces away from the television. While there, she aimlessly flipped through the channels because her parents had finally joined the twenty-first century and gotten cable. Then, she remembered she had forgotten to call her brother, and could only imagine the amount of panic he was experiencing just then, wondering what could have happened to her. He was always the type to run through all the worst possible case scenarios in his mind before discovering everything was perfectly fine. This was a quality that she loved about him, even though, it served to get on her nerves at times. Tessa pulled out her phone and text him that she had made it home safely and that because he was so late getting there, she had already gotten into the left over pot pie their mother had waiting for them in the fridge. "Snooze you lose!" She told him with a pointing finger emoji and a smiley face with its tongue sticking out. Tessa laughed to herself victoriously and settled in for a night of binge watching reruns of Friends or Spongebob, until such a time as he could finally grace them with his presence. But that hour would never come.

As the night went on, Tessa found herself becoming like her brother and going over all of the worst possible case scenarios of what could have happened, and turns out she was correct. They received a call mid-morning of the next day, finally, that her brother's car had been found. He had gotten into a collision with an eighteen wheeler. The authorities explained to them that it was just one of those flukes. A combination of the worst possible situations at the same time that they had seen in a long time. The driver of the eighteen wheeler had been driving for more than sixteen hours, so he was very tired, and eventually fell asleep at the wheel. And, her brother had just received a text message on his phone just a few seconds before the crash, as far as they could gather from the time stamp on the message. So when the driver of the truck swerved into the lane of oncoming traffic, where Geoffrey was in the lead, there was only a split second of time that could have saved him if he had just moved out of the way. But he was too busy looking at his phone to notice the oncoming truck or have the where with all to save himself in the nick of time.

Tessa paused for a moment in-between sips of the hot dark liquid, feeling the steam that rose from the cup waft onto her face, as she felt something entirely different wash over her just then. It was feelings of guilt and wondering if it had been her text message that sent him to his death. They never did tell her whether it had been her fault or not, so she was left to spend the rest of her life in curious torment and wishing she had not messaged him at all. Perhaps, things would have been better and turned out much different if she had decided to stay behind and wait for him to go with her to their mom and dad's, like he had practically begged her to. But she didn't feel it was the smart thing to do because she was already out anyway, and it would have been silly to drive all the way back to campus, just to have to go all the way back in the other direction. Over the next several weeks after that, she wished she had listened to what she used to think of as whining, then more than ever. Even now, as she stood alone in the kitchen, with the time for her to get ready for work ticking away behind the black out of day, dreaming her own thoughts; she still wished as she did then that she had listened. She promised herself that she would never make that mistake with anyone ever again.

Tessa shook her head and wiped the tears that threatened to drip down her face, as she took another sip of her coffee and scurried to the bathroom. She quickly made it into the small room that made her feel like the builders had just shoved a walk in shower into a half bath floor plan. But it served its purpose. Even though, on many evenings, she found herself missing the small luxury of getting to soak in an actual bath tub. She slowly removed her well-worn, spaghetti strap, powder blue sleep shirt and her plaid pajama shorts that had very obviously seen better days. As she threw them into the small bamboo hamper in the corner, she made a mental note to pick up some new things to sleep in, and probably some new underwear. Tessa sighed aloud as she tossed them in the hamper as well. She began to feel she had really let herself go since the breakup with Tedd.

Turning on the shower, she got in and turned the water to her preferred temperature, allowing the cascading flow from the shower head to pour over her slender frame. While the heated waterfall ran down her hair and over her face, she listened to the sound of the droplets fall to the hard, plastic flooring, and it filled her mind with the memories of one of the worst days of her life. In her mind's eye, she could see herself standing there by her brother's grave site. Many random elderly family members had done their best to comfort her and her parents, by telling them that the rain was a good sign. It meant that her brother had been welcomed into the gates of heaven. Tessa felt that if she didn't know any better, she would have believed it. But she was too pragmatic a person to take too much stock in omens and portends. This was yet another memory that felt as if it had happened as recently as yesterday. She recalled how Tedd had been at her side from the beginning of the terrible tragedy that shattered her life. He was so tender and so caring that she couldn't help but find herself falling for him, and seeing him as more than he was. In many ways, she also blamed herself for the fact their relationship even began.

Perhaps, if she had been more in her right mind. Maybe, if she had been in a better place emotionally, this situation would not have occurred at all. Most likely if she had not been so consumed by her pain, she would not have given into his invitation of a one night stand, that ended up transforming into something that ultimately wasted six months of her life.

Only two months after they had gotten together, he convinced her to move in with him. She jumped at the opportunity. However, now that she had the time to think about it, she knew it was because she had landed this great job with the Stafford Financial Group. When she moved in with him, she thought it was just the beginning of a great new chapter in her life. She wasn't thinking about the fact that he was merely using her as a way to boost his financial status, enough to move him out of his parent's basement while he interned as a sous chef for no pay. What was she thinking? Tessa asked herself silently.

Not to mention, just when she thought nothing worse could shock her as much as, if not more than the death of her brother, she discovered it could. On her return home from work that Friday evening, she heard the notification of a text message chiming from her phone in the passenger seat beside her. Tessa made the choice to wait until she arrived home to take a look at it. She figured it was just probably something from her boyfriend telling her how much he was looking forward to her arrival, and all the things he planned for them to do that weekend. They usually involved her spending money she didn't have, to go out with him and their mutual friend from school, Kirsten. And, usually on these outings, she felt more like a third wheel or some kind of glorified chaperone taking out two high schoolers, rather than his girlfriend. She told herself many times after the break up that this should have been her first red flag. But she was too consumed with the fact that she was even in a relationship, that she didn't pay attention. Or maybe she just ignored the signs because she thought that somehow, if she looked away long enough, the problem would just go away.

Like with so many other things, this was however not the case.

As she pulled up in the driveway of their quaint little three bedroom house, she brought the vehicle to a complete stop before reaching over to retrieve her phone from the passenger seat. She knew that nothing could happen to her once she was in the driveway, but the anxiety inspired by her brother's death had made her paranoid enough to wait until she was completely stopped wherever she was, before looking at her phone. When she picked up the device and finally unlocked her screen, she saw that the notification was actually from Kirsten. This didn't really cause her to think anything was amiss, until she opened the message. Her eyes grew wide with dismay as her vision panned over the image like a slow motion camera, taking in the entirety of the picture that awaited her in the message; which was apparently not meant for her. There Kirsten was in all of her nude glory, her freshly spray tanned bare body, and firm, perky breasts on full display. Tessa's eyes trailed her long locks of sandy blonde, chunky, highlighted hair, as they led down to the newly shaved space between her former best friend's legs. The caption of the message read, "Ready and waiting for you Teddy Bear."

Tessa felt a surge of horror and disgust rush through her whole body, causing her to shiver and cast the phone back into the passenger seat, as if she had just touched something utterly horrid. Her head spun as the rest of her world came crashing down around her ears. She was disoriented and heartbroken, completely unsure of what action to take next. All she could think to do was run away as quickly and far away as she could. And, that is exactly what she did. Tessa found herself driving around aimlessly until she made it back into the city, and eventually came upon the welcoming neon lights of a little hole in the wall dive bar. A place where no one knew her, and where she was not in danger of embarrassing herself in front of people who could tell stories about her at work the next day, just in case she happened to get too drunk. Which is what she figured would most likely happen, and she didn't care one bit.

Going into the establishment, she pulled up a stool at the bar; where she found a friendly face that belonged to her now friend, Shalena. At the time, she served as a bit of a taunt to Tessa with her fit, petite frame and bright blonde hair. She noticed that the cut and color of her hair was way better than that bitch Kirsten's. She found out later that everything about Shalena was completely natural, because she was well on her way to getting her degree in sports medicine, and was just serving at the bar to pay for living expenses and college until she got it. She was a woman with goals who had her eye on a job training some sort of Olympic team, soon after getting out of college. She lived on her own, and her entire persona spoke loudly to the fact that she was doing just fine without a man in her life. She was obviously interested in girls, but this didn't matter or really make a difference to Tessa at the moment. She felt herself beginning to experience a slight tinge of envy towards Shalena, even though, she had only just met her. She desired to be as strong, independent, and in control of her own destiny, as this beautiful capable young woman seemed to be. Why couldn't she be like that?

Shalena became a bit of a mother to her over the course of the night, as she listened to Tessa rattling on about the events that had led her to this place in the city; where it was obvious she didn't go often. "Especially, not in those duds." Shalena had commented. But she didn't fault her for her difference in social position or the fact she was a little out of place. She was very understanding and comforting, making her feel like everything would be okay. She would be able to pick up the pieces and move on eventually, on her own, able to take the reins of the course of her life like her new friend had.

By the end of the night, Tessa was quite drunk. Many of the older biker type of gentlemen had jokingly offered to take her off of Shalena's hands, to which she told them to "fuck off" and she would see them tomorrow. This was all Tessa really could remember of that night only a few months ago. The rest of it was a bit of a blur as she made her way to leave the bar, while Shalena was closing up. She told her to wait up because she was in no condition to drive, she tried to protest, only to discover that her keys had been taken by the capable bar tender without her noticing. Tessa had no choice but to follow her directions. This, she eventually found out to her great comfort, involved taking her home to her apartment, to dry out and sleep off her night of drunkenness. She awoke to a monstrous hang over and the terrible overwhelming realization that she had nowhere to live now. Shalena came in shortly after bearing gifts of Krystals burgers, chili cheese fries, and aspirin; as well as the proposition to become her roommate. After talking it over for a little while, it didn't sound like such a bad idea to Tessa, and she accepted almost immediately. She thought about how it wouldn't really be so bad for her to take a break from being around men for a while, except for the occasional few she had to deal with at work. At least this way she could live more autonomously and get back on her feet. Not to mention, she could get some of Shalena's influence to rub off on her while she was at it.

Tessa stood in the mirror of her room for a moment, staring deeply into her own eyes, as she reassured herself that these were the reasons why she was here. This is why she was doing life without a relationship right now, other than a somewhat close friendship with another very productive woman. Her life had taken many turns to lead her to this point which was not altogether very pleasant, but no matter, she was here now, and would live in the present, one day and step at a time; until she achieved her goal. As she carefully and purposefully pulled on her gray, double breasted, single button blazer, she brushed the phantom dust from the shoulders. Looking deeply into her own eyes once again, she told herself that she was already well on her way to doing just that. Tessa had started as an accounting intern at the Stafford Financial Group on Wall Street in her last year of college. They had become so impressed with her abilities as an analyst, that it took her no time at all to be hired as a full time paid employee, becoming a first floor accounting analyst with her own desk within only six months of working there. This gave her a great confidence boost, especially when she began to feel down in the dumps about how stupid she was to date Tedd. When these thoughts would begin to creep out of the quiet recesses of her mind, she would look herself in the eyes and tell herself how capable, strong, and fierce she was; that she was a force to be reckoned with.

Tessa grabbed her leather shoulder bag from off of the small kitchen table as she walked out the door, and locked it tight behind her. She had only a limited window of time before she needed to be on the train to the financial district, if she was going to make to work on time. Once again, she felt she had wasted too much time blacking out in her own thoughts of the past. She was really going to have to find something else to do in the mornings besides that, something more productive. Shalena had recommended that she get up earlier and practice meditation or some kind of exercise regime, which would be fine if she didn't value her sleep so very much. She really needed to come up with some kind of a solution, but the only thing she could think of was to just completely and utterly throw herself into her work. Maybe even to the extent of bringing it home with her like the others did. She knew that would most likely be the best course of action, seeing as how completely immersing herself in the world of figures, equations, and spreadsheets had never failed to help her in the past. Numbers never lied, and as long as she stuck with numbers, they would never let her down. Especially, when it came to focusing her mind into a productive vein.

Tessa made her way through the stampeding multitude of the morning crowd as she crossed the busy street, being sure to put out her hand to stop any oncoming cabs from running her over. She thanked her lucky stars that she was in a line of work that allowed her to wear sensible flat shoes, instead of being required to wear any kind of heels. She couldn't imagine how much difficulty that would add to her trek to work in the mornings. Not to mention, the murder it would most likely be on her feet on the walk home in the evenings. Tessa was not the kind to milk the clock at night, playing solitaire after hours on her computer, to take advantage of the policy to take the company car home. Once this policy had been put in place, many of her coworkers felt they could abuse it. But not Tessa, she was determined to follow the rules at all costs.

She looked over the sea of swaying faces on the subway, as the smell of various people's body odor and their greasy fast food breakfasts crept into her nostrils, causing her to wrinkle her nose slightly. Tessa did her best not to sneeze, she hated doing things like that in public. All of these things compiled like a list in her head, confirming all the reasons why pursuing a relationship with her job was so much more advantageous than pursuing one with another person. You never have to worry about numbers getting smelly, being unreliable, and again, probably the best of all, numbers can't lie to you. Something she valued most above all was honesty. She supposed this was why she was so eager to jump at the opportunity to live with Shalena. She had proven herself to be an honest person above all else, and Tessa needed this in her life more than ever, knowing from experience that she would surely never find this in a man.

Tessa finally reached the end of the line where she saw the sign that she had ultimately reached her destination. She made her way up the steps, careful not to be knocked down by the crowd doing their best to rush to a job they were most likely about to be late for. Good thing she had decided to get up at the time of morning she had, because she still had enough time to walk at a brisk but calm pace. This continued until she reached an opening leading to the bustling street above ground. Here, she could see with greater definition, the towering structures of glass and steel that buffeted the nearly full morning sunlight. As she poured out with the rest of the work force, very much reminiscent of cattle rushing through an open gate, she felt the whip of the wind on her face from the racing vehicles on the street adjacent to the top of the landing. This made her very glad that the entrance to her designated building was not that far away from here. Being careful to cross yet another busy street, she made her way over in an agile jog to the other side and finally to the awaiting glass revolving doors. A sigh of relief escaped her as she made it inside that towering structure, with its gleaming marble floors and sterile chic interior decorating style. Everything was an orgy of evidence that this was meant to be a place of business, and not just any business. The people that ran this corporation were not here to play, they were here to win and they wanted to be assured above all else that the rest of the world understood this very clearly. And, as an employee, she had to make sure that she held herself to the same standard of excellence at all times.

Marching her way confidently to the front desk, she greeted the security guard and the day receptionist as she signed herself into the book, and scanned her name badge. Then, she quickly walked to the elevator and piled in with the rest of her colleagues that all stood perfectly erect, like a troupe of foot soldiers awaiting deployment orders. This part of the morning always made her feel like her posture was a little less than up to snuff, so she often found herself adjusting the straightness of her back as she stood beside her colleagues.

The doors opened and everyone marched out in near perfect lines, much like the march of well-trained militia, all filing to their designated areas of the first floor. Tessa found this to be kind of ironic considering they were actually on the second floor of the building, but no one else seemed to find that funny, so she usually kept what she felt were dorky jokes like that to herself. Walking out onto the floor, she made her way down the aisle that was bordered by a line of desks which were quickly being populated by others in her position. She shared a few cordial smiles and 'good mornings' with her colleagues as she passed them on the way to her designated area. She had made it very easy to spot from the ocean of bland, black painted desks, with a small flowering succulent plant, seated in a decorative pot her mother had gotten her from a trip to Arizona with her father. It filled her with a mixture of happiness and sadness every time she sat down at her desk, like now, because her mother had had a picture from their last family trip together imprinted onto the outer glass of the pot. Tessa sat there for a moment and looked at the picture, as she lovingly caressed the respective faces of her family who she missed very much, lingering a little longer with well-manicured fingers on the smiling face of her brother. She mused about how he was truly happy there, and hoped in spite of herself that he was as happy wherever he was now.

Tessa's eyes moved over to the stack of ledgers that sat atop the center of her desk, beckoning for her to get started on them. This was yet another reason that she had contemplated getting an earlier start here in the mornings, so she wouldn't have to come in to such a mountain of work before she even got here. She stopped admiring the faces of her family and let out a sharp exhale, as she ran the fingers of her other hand through her hair. Reaching into the left hand breast pocket of her blazer, she pulled out her dollar store reading glasses and put them on her nose as someone would put on their game face in preparation for a match. Tessa shook out her hands and grabbed the silver, slim line, black gel ink pin that sat perfectly aligned with the writing guard lying under the mound of ledgers in front of her. She was ready as she was ever going to be to take on the work of the day now.

Smiling to herself and taking one last scan of the room, she took comfort in the fact that she was in her second home, and she was more capable to take on the tasks ahead of her alone, than she was with anyone else.

CHAPTER 2

Trust Fund Babies

———— • ————

The day had begun to fade and had given birth to a humid Spring night. Bryson Stafford's Dolce & Gabbana loafers scuffed through the shiny silver-plated revolving doors, as he walked out of them and into the city streets with a confidence like he owned them. His gaze panned upwards, taking in the entirety of the towering monuments of steel and glass, and to the gods of finance that seemed to penetrate the thick cover of clouds, in the ever darkening night sky. They shimmered in the mingled light of the moon and strategically placed street lights, as distant sirens wailed their ominous calls of possible death and destruction. The whoosh and scrape of tires also breaking the sound barrier, as they sped past on the busy street in front of him.

A scattered multitude of business men were in various states of movement as they yelled unintelligibly into their cell phones, while other people laughed and carried on. They translated to Bryson's wandering mind as different dialects of his own language. A crisscrossing of garbled white noise entering his ears through the smoggy claustrophobic atmosphere. All sensations joining together in a glorious disjointed symphony, all to say for that second, he was alive. For that second, he had completely forgotten the impending doom that he feared would befall him that night. He paused for a moment to mourn the loss of all of his partying playboy days, for he was sure they would soon be a thing of the past if his father dropped the news bomb he feared he would tonight. There was no other reason why he would have convened this super top secret meeting, if not to tell him that he was handing him the company and that he would have to get serious now. This caused Bryson to pout a little, but he figured it would be well worth it. Because there would be no way that he would just let his father hand the family company over to his little brother, Theo, even if he was probably the more capable man for the job. The Stafford Financial Group was like most corporations on Wall Street, they came from old money. It had been around for well over a hundred years and he planned to keep it that way if he could. A business that was the closest thing in the twenty-first century to a kingdom or a dynasty and it was meant to be passed from father to eldest son, just as they did it in the olden days. And, by rights, with Bryson being the eldest of his father's two living sons, he should be the one to get it.

Suddenly pulling his attention from the recesses of his own musings, the sound of tires rushing to a stop at the curb entered his consciousness; signifying Tom's arrival. The sound of Bryson's loafers marching against the concrete joined the collective orchestra fading behind him on his way to the large, black sedan.

"Good evening, sir! Another long hard day at work, or were you hardly working as usual?" Tom quipped as he volunteered his assistance by opening the car door.

"What do you mean, Tom? What I do can kind of be called work, if you call milling around the business and showing everyone my smiling face. That can get very exhausting, you know? Not to mention, I've got to lug around this briefcase and pretend like I was interested in spending fifty something hours on this new deal for Mr. Gates. Which, apparently, I'm supposed to attend a meeting for at precisely eight in the morning, tomorrow. Yeesh!" Bryson informed him in a rambling fashion, as he shoved a heavily loaded leather briefcase into the back seat of the beast of a car. Sliding into the seat beside it, he slammed the heavy door shut with a forceful thud.

"Yes, sir, Mr. Bryson. Sounds like you have a lot of fun lined up for tomorrow. As far as I have been told, you have a little bit of fun lined up for you tonight, up at the big house." Tom acknowledged over his right shoulder from the driver's seat.

"You have no idea," responded Bryson, sighing heavily and settling down into the seat even further, rubbing his tired eyelids with two fingers.

They began to pull away from the curb, and soon joined the crawling herd of other vehicles on the bustling night street. It promised to be a long, arduous frustrating ride to his father's house, and probably an even worse ride home. Bryson felt the sudden anxiety that he didn't have time for this. "Yeah, hey Tom. Would you mind taking a different route to the house this time? Go Broadway to South Street and then down. They're saying there will be less traffic down that way tonight. It might make it a little easier on you." Bryson instructed, beginning to rub what he felt was his prematurely wrinkling forehead as the only way he knew to abate his rising anxiety, while he looked out the window.

"Okay, Mr. Bryson, no worries. I know the way very well. Thanks for the tip. Lord knows ain't nobody got time for that." Tom replied, making a quick, sharp U-turn and flipping the volume to Moby's "Natural Blues". It seemed to play louder and louder as the shiny black town car powered down through the concentrated block of marble and granite.

With one finger, Bryson frustratedly unbuttoned the top button of his stress wrinkled, blue pin-striped button up Oxford shirt, then pressed his finger to the window. Swap spreads, convexities, durations, and crack spreads exploded in his head in a dancing chorus of confusion from hell. They felt as if they had begun to trickle out of his sweaty finger and onto the humidity fogged glass of the back passenger seat window. He felt like a college kid that was having to cram some kind of crash course, in something he was utterly unfamiliar with, for a test he needed to ace tomorrow, or worse, in the next five minutes. But he had to find some way to fake it until he could make it. He needed desperately to make his father see that he was making the right decision to leave the company in his hands. Even though he did not feel the most able at the moment, he was sure he would learn in time, or find some kind of damn good accountant that he could make his right hand man. One who would make him look good in front of everyone else. If only his father hadn't been so hell bent on making sure that he was a leader rather than a boss. He had never been satisfied with making everyone else under him do all of the grunt work, and just living off the fat of their spoils, without having participated in any of the cultivation. Abram Stafford was quite the formidable businessman, a force to be reckoned with on Wall Street, a survivor of the Great Recession of '08, and he was going to be damn sure that everyone knew about it. Bryson would always laugh to himself about how his father should have had t-shirts made to the same effect and just be done with it, instead of telling every person he felt would listen the harrowing tale.

Apparently, it had not been that harrowing, Bryson thought to himself. Unlike the other people around them who were much less fortunate, neither his family nor anyone at the company really suffered any major losses when the market crashed. Some people had to not only downsize their staff, but some of them either had to begin outsourcing their labor to other countries, or just shut down altogether. The affected would then be left having to run for the sparse jobs of the blue collar sector, never to be heard from again. Many more were even worse off, having been found out for cooking the books before the big crash and contributing to the bubble. And so, inevitably, the government came knocking on their doors, and now they were doomed to spend the rest of their days in club fed. Not such a bad prospect, honestly, Bryson mused with a curve of his lip and raise of his eyebrow. He pictured all of those old men in jump suits getting free food, free health care, and getting to play golf whenever they wanted. Was that really so bad? Could that really be called punishment? He wasn't sure, but he knew this is just the way the world worked. It was a world that he was very accustomed to, much like this street he was looking out upon through the window. This street was as close and familiar as a brother to him. It provided a strange sense of constancy and security for him every time he found himself on it, while at the same time creating a sense of fear and trepidation within his core that he could explain very well. As they continued to drive along, he did his best to distract himself from this realization, and his vision honed in on the sight of a young man standing on the crowded but lonely street corner, next to the big auburn bronzed bull. A hard sigh escaped from Bryson's heavy chest, as he observed yet another moderately good looking man that reminded him a lot of himself when he was just a bit younger. A green sort of fellow, obviously fresh out of college, his dad had probably gotten him an interview with some big financial corporation. He most likely hated Wall Street and longed to be in some other line of work, but had been so badly brain washed that he had forgotten all about that and joined the cult of the marching coins, leaving no room in his life for anything else but trading stocks. And he probably did so like he was in pursuit of some Holy Grail. Deep down, he was really a good guy underneath, which is most likely what he told himself in the mirror every night to help him sleep. But on the outside he was just another well dressed, villainous, fat cat that we all loved to hate. Also, as was customary with all people in his position, his pupils were the size of a dime because of his constant diet of caffeine, nicotine, and whatever else it was that he just happened to be taking at the time, to keep himself awake. Or from having to face those rare, quiet moments alone before going to sleep. Moments where those dark thoughts creep out from wherever you had them buried in the deep recesses of your mind. Include with this are all those little voices that fill you with self-doubt, and make you feel like the loser that you probably are when you boil everything down. But if there is no reason for sleep, you never have to worry about finding yourself in that position. Besides, who sleeps anymore now days. Wasn't that something that only trended in the circles of pussies and dead people? At least, that is what Bryson always thought. It was just something that was cooked up by lazy people who were still satisfied with playing small, and found pleasure in their never ending black hole of never ending laziness. He knew those kind of people all too well, for he had been compared to one all his life by his brother, Theo. He was always trying to outdo him at everything. Bryson supposed this constituted normal behavior between brothers, but at times he felt that if he had the chance he most certainly would have slit his throat while he was sleeping. No, that would have been too quiet and simple. He would need to find something more spectacularly public and humiliating. This is why Bryson would be sure to watch his back once his father gave the company over to him. No more random women that could possibly be bought off to create some sort of scandal at his expense.

Bryson was not sure if it was because he had been so consumed by his own day dreaming, but it did not seem like it took them very long to arrive at his father's house. The iron gate leading up to the long driveway of his father's spacious living quarters, opened slowly and almost ominously. The sound of the whining hinges made its way through the closed window into the cab of the vehicle, and finally into Bryson's ears, causing him to cringe slightly. That would be attended to he was sure, but not right now. There were too many other things that took top priority just at the moment. This train of thought moved Bryson's hand to involuntarily take his brief case and have it at the ready for his dart out of the car. Suddenly, with all of his anxiety about pleasing his father and taking over the company, he felt he needed to have some kind of head start.

As soon as the vehicle came to a stop, he opened the door and flew out in a speed that made it seem like he had teleported outside onto the pavement of the driveway. He turned and barely peered at Tom through the divide of the driver's and front passenger seats from his view through the open back side door.

"Is this good night, Mr. Bryson? Or would you like me to wait and give you a ride home?" Tom's voice sounded calm and very matter of fact, which confused Bryson because of the slightly befuddled and worried look on his face. Perhaps, it was the stern expression that Bryson felt would take up permanent residence on his face, that caused his own voice to take on an octave pitch higher than was normal for a man his age.

"Be here..." Bryson stopped to clear his throat momentarily, once he noticed the strange sound of his words. "Yeah, Tom, you can go ahead and wait for me here. If that is alright? I'm sure you've had a long day."

"That's no problem, Mr. Bryson. I'm just doing my job." Responded Tom, with a two fingered salute in Bryson's direction.

"Alright, I'll be out if they don't kill me first." Bryson tried to soften his harsh expression with a slight smile. His reciprocating of the two finger salute with his own made Tom laugh at him a little bit.

Bryson closed the door slowly, being sure not to slam it this time as he had done before. He needed to prove to himself more than anyone else that he could be calm and collected under pressure, even though right at this moment, he felt he would have to play at it until it became a reality. What would get him through the next hour or so until he could get home to his warm bed was fine with him, just as long as this whole process would be over soon, and he would have the keys to the kingdom.

Bryson made his way up the familiar stone steps that led up to the double wrought iron storm doors that used to intimidate him so much as a child. They didn't seem quite so tall now as they did when he was younger, but now they were still just as fearful, if not more so.

He punched in the familiar code and let himself in. His father's household had finally moved into the modern age with an up to date security system, and forgotten all the hassle of manual locks with keys that have a bad habit of getting lost. Once inside the small entryway, he walked slowly towards the vast foyer that nearly made up the entire lower level of the house, and found himself standing on a black and white tile floor that led to the landings of an expansive, towering staircase, spiraling in opposite directions. The house seemed empty, and felt almost hollow at the lack of people in it. There were usually a lot more people walking around throughout the house; various members of staff and one or two of his father's wives that he just couldn't bear to be paired with. He thought about how his father was the worst case scenario of a person that liked to take in strays of all kinds, everything from animals to human beings. Anyone with a hard luck story and a sad, puppy dog look on their face, and he was convinced that he was the only one that could help them. That wasn't so bad, he guessed, there were worse things he could be into he was sure; that would probably make him look a lot worse to the public. Bryson hoped his father did not see this kind of behavior as a requirement of his taking over the company.

He began to cautiously walk up the stairs like a man on the way to his impending execution. He tried to calm himself, for he didn't understand why he was taking this as seriously as he was. He knew his father was going to give him the company anyway. All of this ominous late night meeting was just a formality, a way to keep his brother from making some kind of a scene that could be witnessed by their employees during the day.

"And, look who finally decided to grace us with his presence." Bryson's ears were suddenly assaulted by the sound of his brother Theo's voice. He looked up, startled out of his own thoughts and musings, to take in the image of his brother's snidely smiling face. The sharpness of his features with his pointed nose, high, deep cut, jutting cheek bones and firm jawline, served only to make him look even more predatory. His bright, large aquamarine eyes and flaming red hair gave Bryson the feeling that he was staring at an oversized leprechaun every time he saw his brother. Except this time, it was a little different. Theo's expression held the same vibe as that of a cat who has eaten the canary and was very proud of it. This filled Bryson even more with that nagging sense of foreboding that he had carried from the office to the house, and it seemed to be growing stronger by the minute. He wished for them to see their father and hurry up and get this over with, so he could smack that smarmy look off of his brother's face.

"I was busy. There's a lot of details that need to be taken care of back at Stafford before in the morning." Bryson replied.

"Translation, there are a lot of things you are still unfamiliar with because you decided to squander your time on fast cars and fast women, rather than learning the business. I told you, you would regret it all one day, when the time came." Theo called over his shoulder as he began to lead

Bryson down the long corridor that led to their father's room. "But if my calculations are correct," he said grabbing the door knob before letting Bryson in. "You may not even have to worry about it at all, and you will be able to go back to your little land of parties and behaving like the money just grows on trees, or flows into your trust fund from some magical unknown place."

Bryson's mouth shot open, he was prepared to counter Theo's words and defend himself, but before he even had the chance, Theo smiled and flung the door open. He glided in before Bryson could step in the door and he watched from behind like he was watching a snake slither across the floor towards his father. He made his way in as well and closed the door behind him. When he turned around, he saw that his father had risen to a standing position from the high backed leather chair that faced the balcony, making it seem as if he had appeared in the room out of nowhere.

Even as a rapidly aging man with a bone disease that had stolen some of his height, Abram Stafford still possessed the presence of a man who was a force to be reckoned with. There was no mistaking from the harsh lines that were carved into his face, his large deep set eyes, and still jet black hair that was only dappled with lines of gray and white; just enough to tell everyone he had not dyed it. All of it told a story of a young man who had lived a long, hard life, and hadn't let it phase his attitude or allowed it to wear him down in the slightest.

He opened his arms wide and reached for Bryson, to pull him into a customary bear hug. For such a serious man, his father was still a very loving and encouraging sort. The only salve to the harshness of his severe demands for such a high standard of excellence in life, that Bryson was sure he had failed to achieve. But he was going to make the most of this opportunity being handed to him by his father, to prove that he could be responsible and make him proud before it was too late.

"Here, come take a seat, my sons." Abram gestured to the other two chairs that sat with their backs to the balcony and faced their father's chair. Theo blew past him and sat down in the chair he felt was closest to his father, while Bryson was satisfied to sit a small distance away. They sat there in an awkward silence for a moment, as their father looked over them like he was examining the expressions on their faces. Once he seemed satisfied with what he saw he began to speak.

"I know you are both pretty certain about why I have called this meeting tonight. I apologize for the hour, but my sleep schedule is not what it used to be. I have had to take to listening to my body rather than it just being satisfied with me being in charge. Old age," he sighed and pointed at the both of them. "Avoid it if at all possible."

Theo chuckled slightly, and Bryson did his best to follow suit, but it came out more as a small burst of nervous laughter that he did not anticipate. His father looked over the both of them once more, his gaze lingering on Bryson a little longer than he would have liked, and it caused him to want to squirm uncomfortably in his chair, but he restrained himself to the best of his ability.

"Neither of you have any cause for being uncomfortable, this is just a friendly chat. A chance for me to tell you the way your lives are about to change. You see, I am very proud of the men that you have both become, granted you have been through some rough spots that we have had to iron out. A little bit more effort had to be applied to one more than the other." Abram shot a glance over to Bryson when he said this, and he could feel the burning of his brother's gloating smile when he noticed this.

"But, all of that is in the past, and we must now concentrate on the future. Even though, there are great lessons to be learned from our history. You come from very strong working stock and I expect you to do your best to continue to remember and respect that over the course of the rest of your lives. Especially, as you carry on the tasks with which I am about to set before you." He instructed.

"And what would those be, Father?" Asked Theo, as if he already knew what the answer was going to be, but he knew that the revelation would cause Bryson to possibly feel more uncomfortable.

"Patience, my son, I am getting to that. As you know, you have been blessed far and above what I was allowed in the beginning of my life." Abram began and Bryson felt the customary feeling of dread that he usually felt, whenever his father was about to go into the long story of his rise to victory; one which he had heard over a hundred times he was sure.

"Unlike the two of you, I did not have the luxury of getting to know my father from a young age. My father abandoned me to face the cruel world of man when I was but six years old, during the time of the Great Depression. This left my mother a widow with seven children to feed and care for. The only choice she had left was to send most of us to a group home, and my eldest sister of twelve had to pretend that she was much older, so she could get a job as a waitress in a neighboring state and send her pay home; until such a time as they could raise enough money to rescue us from the system. This bred a lot of anger and resentment from my eldest brother, Addison, who protected me from many horrors that were to be found in the group home, until we were able to return to our mother, and caused him to die very young from a heart attack. I became the eldest son and man of the house at the ripe old age of ten. It was then and there that I vowed to myself that I would not let my family continue to live in squalor ever again. So, I persevered, just as my mother did, founding four restaurants while still a single mother, until she met my step father at the counter of one of her diners. Many would think that it was just chance for her to have met a financial tycoon that fateful afternoon. But as we all know, there are no such things as coincidences. Papa Stafford became my father, saw my potential for running a successful business from a young age, and taught me everything I know and more. This is the gift that I hope I have been able to bestow upon the two of you in my long life, as well as the vitality to not follow in the footsteps of the other men in my family and die young. I only suggest you try to do better than me, and not live so long they discover things about your genetics they could only know if someone lives to my age." Abram posited.

“Oh, yes, about that. What did your oncologist say when you went for your appointment today?” Theo asked with feigned concern.

“That is another thing that I wanted to discuss with the two of you. The reason I have called this meeting.” Abram responded.

“What do you mean, father?” Bryson sat up ready to rush to his father’s side as he felt a sudden shock surge through him.

“Well, if you had decided to be here a little more often and attend to father as the rest of us have, you would know these things.” scolded Theo.

Abram raised his hand and patted the air before his other son as if to stamp the rising tide of contention. “Now, now, I do appreciate your concern. But there is no need for all of that, Theo. Your brother does what he can, as he is able. Besides, it’s not something that many people know yet. So, it only stands to reason that this would be first he is hearing about it as well.” Bryson’s father smiled a reassuring smile in his direction, doing his best to comfort him.

“So, what did they say? Are you dying?” Bryson could feel a strain coming over his voice, and he tried to restrain the lump he felt growing in the terrified throat.

“First things first,” he raised his hand once again, before taking a sip of the whiskey that sat in a tumbler on the small table beside his chair. “If you must know, the answer to both of your questions, is yes I did speak with the doctor today. And, yes, as far as they can tell I may not last much longer. It would seem that my bout of prostate cancer that they thought would just be taken care of with a little outpatient radiation has turned out to be a lot more aggressive than they anticipated.” Abram looked over the shocked and horrified expressions of both sons before beginning to speak again. “It has made it to my bladder and they tell me it will only be a matter of time before it has metastasized to the rest of my bones and organs. This is why time is of the essence, and we must set things in motion, in preparation for the future of our family and our company.

You understand now, don't you, the full gravity of the situation we find ourselves in?"

"Yes, father." Theo and Bryson nearly said in unison. Bryson found his words coming out in almost a whisper as he felt someone had utterly knocked the wind out of him. There was a clinching pain in his chest to match. But as he looked over to Theo, he began to wonder why he was not as shocked as he, then again he had never really possessed any kind of sensitivity. This made him wonder if he was really their father's son at all at times.

"So, now that we have gotten those pleasantries out of the way, down to business. I have come with a plan that I know may make the both of you a little displeased with me, but I feel that it is necessary to see which would be the most capable of taking on this task that lies ahead of the both of you after I am gone. I have made provisions for the both of you to respectively take over my position as CEO of Stafford Financial Group. Bryson,"

Bryson looked up from his hands and intensely into his father's eyes.

"I will have you be the first to take over for the first quarter in my place, and we will see how you fare after this trial. After, I will allow your brother to run the company as he pleases for the three months after that and once six months has passed, and if I am still here. We will have another meeting and determine which one of you is the best man to take over my empire." Abram finished very matter of factly.

"This sounds like a very fair plan, father." Theo injected into the awkward silence that had fallen over the three of them. "What do you have to say about all of this, Bryson? Does this sound fair to you?" His gaze lingered on Bryson, making him feel like he wanted to crawl out of his skin.

Bryson felt once again like the wind had been knocked out of him, but this time for a completely different reason. This news that his father was not just going to hand the company over to him seemed to shock him even more than the revelation that his father may not live long enough to see the end of the six month trial period. He took a moment to collect his composure and behave as if this earth shattering news did not faze him at all.

"Yes, Theo, it sounds quite fair. As long as you're up to the challenge." Bryson goaded him.

"I would look to myself if I were you, brother of mine. It is not I that I am concerned about being up to the challenge." Theo parried.

Abram stood up slowly from his chair, signifying that he was becoming tired, and he was ready for them to leave. "Alright, boys, save the competition for tomorrow."

Both of the young men stood and straightened their suits before reaching in to hug their father. Theo threw Bryson a glance as he left the room that he knew if looks could kill he would most assuredly died right there on the spot. But before he could concentrate too much of his mental energy on that, his father brought his attention back to him by grasping both of his arms. They looked at each other for a moment longer before his father said, "I am counting on you, son." He firmly patted the outside of his arm.

"Don't worry, father. I won't disappoint you this time."

C H A P T E R 3

Unaccounted For

———— • ————

Tessa worked at a frenzied pace, taking down one file at a time. If her mind had not been so preoccupied, she probably would have noticed long enough to pat herself on the back. But alas, she was too consumed by the rhythm of her work to come to a stop.

She stopped for a moment to take a drink of her coffee she had brought back from lunch, which she didn't really take, because she felt she didn't really have time. Especially with her new formula for getting work done. This included just jumping into it with both feet, and not bothering to come up for air until she was completely finished with everything on her desk, and in the hub. No need to sparse everything out over the course of the week any more, she was going to get herself labeled as the most productive analyst on the floor before the day was over. She was here to win now and she felt this was the best way to do it. Who needs breaks, right? Or sanity? Both of those seemed like pretty overrated sentiments. She could hear her mother now, "you know that's how people end having heart attacks before they're twenty-seven, and end up having to have organs removed, because they can't keep up with how fast you're living."

Tessa took a moment to breath as she surveyed the amount of work that lined the out box of her work hub. She had had a pretty damned productive day if she did say so herself. If she worked anywhere else, there would probably be someone around for her to high five, but this was not that kind of place, and she would just have to be satisfied with high fiving Shalena later at the bar.

She smiled and let out an exhale that came out a lot louder than she anticipated. She looked around a little embarrassed and covered her mouth, hoping no one else had noticed. To her relief, the sparse amount of people that were still here at their desks this late, were too consumed with their work as she had been, to care that someone was making any noise.

Tessa scooted her wheeled office chair back from the desk, to give herself room to open the drawer on her right and remove her leather shoulder bag. She groaned with exhaustion, feeling as if she had just run a marathon of some kind. Or at least she imagined this is what it would feel like if she were into that sort of thing. Maybe, she would add some kind of exercise to her list of deviations that would change her life for the better. Just not right now at least, the thought only served to make her feel even more out of breath.

She stood from her seat and began to turn off the desk lamp, when suddenly there was the dinging sound of an email notification on her desktop computer. Tessa debated with herself for a moment whether she should stay and look at the email. She knew that if she got too far into reading it, she would be consumed once again by the work bug and probably wouldn't get out of work until much later. It wasn't like she didn't need the money, because Lord knows she did. So she decided against the conflicting aching of her muscles to sit down once again and take a look at the email. What could it hurt, right?

Tessa resumed her seat in the desk chair and put her glasses back on as she slid closer to the screen to take a better look at the contents of the files. There were several expense sheets attached to the email which she began to open one by one. She pulled out her pen and her calculator once again and began to process the numbers. Everything seemed to be going as well as could be expected, just your run of the mill expense reports that needed to be filed with payroll, for The Go-To Construction company that was doing some outsourcing for the local memorial hospital. Until suddenly, she seemed to hit some kind of a snag. Tessa figured it was just her tired mind playing tricks on her and her brain was most likely not braining the way it had, earlier on in the work day when it was fresh and caffeinated.

She shook her head and let out a breath as she started the calculations over again. Then, ran them through the accounting software on her computer just to be absolutely certain. To her bewilderment, everything still came out the same way it had before. How could this be possible? There was no way there would be this many discrepancies in a file like this. Especially, not from the Stafford Financial Group. It must have been a mistake from the construction company themselves. But she needed to get a second opinion. So she decided to set off for the office of her department supervisor. Maybe, she could make some sense of all of this. Hopefully she was still there, after all it was very late.

Tessa's sensible black flat pattern leather shoes made quiet slapping sounds, as she walked across the tile floor towards the closed door of her department supervisor's office. Finally making it there, she tried to peer through the cracks in the black blinds that hung on the inside of the windows. She could see that the lights were still on, and that someone appeared to still be seated behind the desk in the small confines of the office. Tessa lightly rapped on the door with her free knuckle.

"Come in," called a middle aged female voice from the other side of the glass door.

Tessa opened the door cautiously and peeked her head in the door way between the door jam and the door.

"Oh, Tessa, hello dear." Mrs. Davis greeted her from behind the desk. She smiled up at her from behind her reading glasses that had slid down her bird like nose. This reminded Tessa very much of her old English teacher, with her gray hair piled on top of her head in a messy sort of bun, and her face that was decorated with deep wrinkles that told the story of how hard her life had been. A tapestry of all of the children she had raised, and long hours she had worked, in order to provide the best possible life for them. Tessa felt this temperament bled over into how she treated everyone here on the first floor. She had always been a very caring, mothering, sort of woman from the time that Tessa arrived, which put her at ease to bring anything up to her that she felt was out of place and she was always gracious to explain it.

"Hi, um...Mrs. Davis, I was wondering if I could trouble you for a moment. I know it's a bit late and you're probably ready to go. But if you could just take a look at this for me, I'm a little stumped." Tessa prevaricated.

Mrs. Davis motioned her inside. "That won't be a problem at all, honey. Let me take a look at it." She replied.

Tessa walked in and closed the door quietly behind her. She made her way around the desk and placed the file in front of the older woman, opening it to the appropriate section. Pointing to the offending figures, she explained, "You see, here is where I am having trouble. I received this in an email a little over an hour ago and I have been wracking my brain to try and decipher it. But it always comes out to that number."

"Hmm," mused Mrs. Davis, pushing her glasses closer to her eyes as she lifted the file folder from the desk to get a better look. She hummed a little under her breath as Tessa watched her eyes move back and forth over the sheet, taking in all of the numbers.

"If this is correct, I think I have stumbled upon something very shady." Tessa injected into the silence that had come over the room.

"What do you mean, dear?" Mrs. Davis looked at her from over the thick rims of her glasses, once again.

"Well, you see here where it talks about the health and wellness accounts?" Tessa touched the section on the page.

"Yes," Mrs. Davis acknowledged, following the line of Tessa's arm to the section.

"If this is correct, key phrase here is 'if this is correct'. This means that all of the money that they say they are placing in these health and wellness accounts for those in security and the contractors for the construction company is not being used for the purpose of health care. They are not even allowing the employees to have access to the money and it is being funneled elsewhere. From the looks of it, in the last six months, it is to the tune of a quarter of a million dollars. Which means…"

"Yes, I am well aware of what that means." Mrs. Davis suddenly cut her off in a tone she had never heard her use before. However, it did not sound so harsh as it sounded more like she was very afraid of something. Tessa figured it was because if this were to get out they would soon have the feds breathing down their necks and that was the last thing any company of their status wanted.

After a long and thoughtful pause, Mrs. Davis removed her glasses altogether and began to chew on the ends. "Tessa, I need you to be completely honest with me."

"Yes, Mrs. Davis." Tessa replied, feeling an overwhelming sense of foreboding. She found herself waiting for the sound of the loud thud of a shoe dropping.

"Have you talked to anyone else about this? Anyone at all?" Mrs. Davis turned to look her intently in the eyes when she asked her. And, Tessa felt that her gaze was boring holes into her soul. This gave her the idea that Mrs. Davis was trying to tell her she would know if she were lying.

"N...no ma'am, no one at all. You are the first person I came to about this." Tessa reassured her in a nervous tone.

Mrs. Davis breathed a heavy sigh of relief and sat back in her chair once again, showing Tessa that she had begun to relax. She took another look at the file. "How did you come to have this in your work hub, anyway?"

"What do you mean?" Tessa asked, turning as she had begun to leave.

"Well, it says in the top right hand corner that this is a file from the third floor. Why do you have it? That's a little advanced for you isn't it?" Mrs. Davis queried and Tessa got the distinct impression that she was trying to make her feel a little stupid or inadequate, like she was some sort of child trying to do things that should only be left for adults. But she chose to brush it off.

"The only reason I even opened it was because it showed up in my inbox." Tessa responded.

"Oh, okay. Well, I wouldn't worry myself too much about it if I were you. This is something that they deal with up on the third floor. So we are probably just taking it out of context." Mrs. Davis spoke as if she was trying to reassure herself more than she was Tessa.

"I hope so," Tessa added.

"It most likely is, dear. As I said, I wouldn't worry any more about it." Mrs. Davis said, punctuating her sentence like she was putting a button on the situation altogether.

Tessa felt it was probably best just to do as she had previously planned and leave for a night at home, where she could forget all of this; at least until tomorrow that is. She turned to make her departure from the office and began to close the door behind her, bidding Mrs. Davis good night as she left. When, just then, Mrs. Davis stopped her with one last word. "Oh, and Tessa."

"Yes, Mrs. Davis?" Tessa looked over her shoulder.

"Due to the fact this was most likely some kind of a fluke, I wouldn't go around mentioning this to anyone else on our floor or anywhere else, alright? It will only lead to a lot of whispering that will just start a big ruckus, which our competition will take advantage of, and it will most likely end in the loss of your job. Neither you nor I would like that to happen now would we?" Tessa could hear the sound of a veiled threat in her words. "You have a promising career ahead of you, and sometimes sacrifices and compromises need to be made in order to further said career. I'm sure you understand."

A slight feeling of righteous indignance rose up within Tessa, and she felt that she would explode all over Mrs. Davis about the importance of honesty and moral integrity. But, she also felt the need to restrain herself just at this moment, until she could get a better handle on the situation. She knew that if there was indeed a real problem, she could have it sussed out by tomorrow and be able to take the evidence to the proper authorities. So it was best to hold her tongue for now.

"I understand very well," Tessa said with a sternness that seemed to surprise both Mrs. Davis and herself. But she held her ground. "Good night," she punctuated her standoff with the older woman very matter-of-factly, and she closed the door to her office.

Tessa did her best to cool off after her little clandestine altercation with her department supervisor. She had the strange feeling she had made it so far into the company she was now to the point where she was well past the honeymoon stage, and her job was going to turn out like her last relationship. She was about to find out all of the dirty little secrets and where all of the bodies were buried, and she was not so sure she would like that. In fact, she was certain she was not going to like it one bit. Especially if it required her to make compromises and allowances for things that would go against the grain of her honest character. Was everything in life this way? She hoped not, or else she was doomed to live the rest of her life as a cynic, and she hated the prospect of that more than anything. Maybe, this was only one part of it and everything was not as bad as she was making it out to be.

When Tessa broke free from the building she once saw as a refuge and sanctuary from all of her other worldly problems, she took a deep breath of the humid spring night air. Feeling the mist on her face that she was sure was not from the dew of night, and was most likely from the rising steam from the man hole covers, that strategically littered the still bustling street awaiting her outside. Tessa did something a little out of character and decided to hail a cab to take her to A Salt and Battery, where Shalena bartended. She hoped that maybe a little small talk between her and the cabbie would distract her enough to clear her head of all the scrambling cobwebs that now filled it. But she was wrong, it did not. All she could think about as she politely listened to snatches of his story about his kids and his aging mother that he was left to care for on his salary, was how The Stafford Financial Group was most likely just another den of thieves; like the others that lined the streets of Wall Street, and she would now be counted as one of them. She was determined to make sure at whatever the cost, that she would be sure not to be lumped in with the rest of them. She was different. A moral person with a strong sense of preserving her character, and what was right and wrong.

Tessa thanked the man for his expedient service and tipped him extra to help with his mother's care. He thanked her profusely in his broken English and told her to call the number on his cab and ask for him personally, if she needed anything else. She made a mental note of it for later as she marched briskly to the door of the dive bar. She needed a drink.

Tessa made it to the single door entrance of the bar, where a large, burly biker gentleman opened the door for her with a smile and a slight quizzical look at her business casual attire. She just smiled cordially and thanked him, as she nearly had to shimmy past him to get into the large room. She looked briefly at the chalk board sign that was written in the all too familiar doctoresque hand writing of her best friend, it read, "Seat Yourselves." Tessa laughed a little at how it was short, sweet, to the point and not in the least bit polite. It was a testament to Shalena's somewhat abrasive personality. She was definitely one of those people that you had to take a moment or two before she would warm up to you. But once you were considered a part of her circle, you were in, and Tessa had a feeling that death was probably the only way out. Which gave her a mixed feeling of fear and reassurance as she thought of it.

"Hey, chickie poo!" Called Shalena from behind the bar, grabbing Tessa's attention from her own consuming thoughts. It was difficult to see more than her waving hand from behind the group of large men who sat at the bar. Shalena was not only a very fit person, but she was also very short. She would be sure to correct you and tell you that she was fun-sized rather than challenged in the height department. This made her appear to be very cute and unassuming, but Tessa knew better than to let this fool her. Shalena was quite the force to be reckoned with, definitely not someone you would want to come across in a dark alley. Unless of course she was defending you.

Tessa walked carefully over the badly scratched and worn hardwood floor, and finally made it to the side of the bar closest to the wall. This was a habit she had learned from her friend. It was safer to sit somewhere in public with your back facing the wall, this way you don't have to worry about people stabbing you in the back. A sentiment that she found to be a little silly, but she was sure to follow her direction and humor her strange friend.

Tessa figured that the expression on her face said everything Shalena needed to know when she took her seat on the bar stool, because Shalena paused almost immediately in the middle of drafting someone a beer, to check on her friend.

"What gives? Hard day at work?" Shalena asked, going back to the task at hand and giving the pint to the awaiting sausage fingers extended in her direction. She made her way over to Tessa and slapped her palms down on the bar in front of her.

Tessa blew out an aggressive breath that filled her cheeks, like a chipmunk that was ready to explode. "You have no idea," she finally blurted out in a tired and sluggish tone.

"Oh, baby. Tell mommy all about it while I get you a drink, okay?" Shalena said grabbing a bottle down from the top shelf and taking it to the blender.

"Oh, baby. Aw." uttered a collective chorus of jeering male voices from around the bar.

Shalena turned on the ball of her foot and pointed in their direction. "I don't recall asking for any input from the peanut gallery. Sounds to me like some people need to get cut off."

There was the sound of yet another set of collective grumbles from the said peanut gallery.

"That's what I thought," stated Shalena with a smile and nod of her head towards Tessa. "Alright now, spill. Well, don't spill, but you know what I mean."

"Well, something very odd happened at work today. I was getting ready to leave and I got an email in my work hub from the third floor, which was the first odd thing. Because I work on the first floor. But I decided what the heck, I'm just going to be nice and go over everything anyway. So that's what I did." Tessa began to explain the events that led to why she was feeling this way now.

"Just like you to do work that isn't yours. Let me guess you got flack for it?" responded Shalena, as she set the watermelon cosmo in front of Tessa.

Tessa gave her a knowing glance from over the top of her glass as she took a sip. The refreshing fruity taste washed over her palette and renewed her vigor. "Well, yeah, but that isn't why."

"Oh, okay. Just know I get to say I told you so the next time things like this come crashing down around your head." She replied with a slight cock of her head to the side.

"I know, I know." Tessa said with a sheepish look as she took another drink. "So, anyway, back to my story. I came across some figures that didn't quite make any sense because it said that the money was going into health and wellness, but the people it was being delegated to aren't allowed to use it."

"Ah, I see." Shalena stated showing that she was absorbing what Tessa was saying, with a look like she already had an idea of what was going on.

"From the looks of things, apparently, this has been going on for the last few months and no one has caught on to it until now. I don't see how, though, because it adds up to about a quarter of a million dollars." Tessa continued to explain.

"Oooh, ouch. Now that's illegal." Shalena blurted out. "How are the feds not involved by now?"

"That's what I'm wondering," answered Tessa. "So I took it to my department supervisor and told her about it, and all she could tell me was that I didn't need to say anything to anyone about it."

"Why the hell not?" asked Shalena.

"Well, she told me that it could cause some kind of undue panic that would ultimately get me fired." Tessa responded.

"Oh, she did, did she now?" Shalena's words oozed out smoothly as if she was planning something sly. "Well, honey, that just goes to show you that you can't trust middle or lower management types. You know, that bitch is probably in on it."

Tessa felt an uncomfortable shudder come over her. "You think so? I mean she's been there practically forever. I would hate to believe that about her. Besides, it's not good to just assume that sort of thing about people."

"Look at you still so innocent," Shalena cooed at her like she was a child. "Oh, honey, those are the worst kind. They think they can get away with shit like this because they have been there so long. So when someone catches onto their little scheme they think because they have manager or supervisor behind their name, they can squelch it by threatening to fire them. I tell you what you do,"

"What?" Tessa sat up closer on the bar, propping her elbows on it as a sign she was listening more intently.

"You take the evidence that you have, and stop messing around with these small time players and go to the big boss. You tell them what's going on, and they will sort it out. That way, if anything does go down, you are not the one responsible for getting anyone fired or investigated. Because, that is another thing. If you keep messing around with these other folks you're going to find a target on your back, and as we both know when there is big money involved; these people don't play." Shalena informed her.

Tessa felt another wave of uneasiness wash over her, but at the same time she experienced a new confidence arise within her. Her friend was right, she needed to gather all of the evidence she could and take it through the proper channels. She began to feel as if a light bulb had turned on over her head, as she started to make a list of all the things she needed to do tomorrow to make this happen.

"Now, enough about work, because you know all work no play makes Jill a dull girl." Shalena's voice piped into her ears dispersing the cloud of her thoughts. Tessa had a slight sense of dread come over her at the sound of these words. She could only imagine what Shalena was about to get her into. Even though they were becoming close friends, the two of them had quite differing ideas on what was fun and what was not.

"Yeah, what did you have in mind?" She asked reluctantly.

"Oh, don't look at me in that tone of voice. You haven't even heard my idea yet." Shalena scolded playfully.

"Okay, what did you have in mind?" Tessa repeated in her best cheerful voice.

"That's better, now do you see that scrumptious morsel seated at the end of the bar?" Shalena motioned as inconspicuously as she could with a swing of her head to the tall gentleman sitting at the end of the bar.

The feeling of dread and reluctance returned. She had been right, her idea of fun and Shalena's were quite different in this case.

"Well, you know, I wouldn't really know about him being a tasty snack, really. But he looks average, you know, not so bad. Plus, I told him I would talk to you for him when you came in." Shalena prodded.

"Ugh, Shalena. No." Tessa replied, bringing Shalena's attention back to her, for she had turned momentarily to wave at the man who smiled back at her in Tessa's direction.

"Oh, but why not? He's kind of cute, right?" Shalena pleaded.

"But I'm not ready. Plus, I have a lot on my plate right now with work. I just don't have the time to add something like that into my life just now." Tessa countered.

"Well, when will you? There's no time like the present to jump back in there, get back on the saddle, test the waters...all that jazz. It's about time you stop letting that jerk Tedd keep you hung up and from living your best life." Shalena countered back.

"He...he...for your information he's not keeping me from living my best life. I'm just having to delegate my priorities a little better right now. And, at this current moment they don't include getting laid, as you call it. I'm waiting for something a little more permanent, a little more worth my time." Tessa snapped firmly, causing her friend to shrink back slightly with the force of her tone.

"Alright, alright, my bad. I just get a bit worried about you sometimes is all. You know I don't suggest anything I don't think would be good for you." Shalena said apologetically putting her hand on Tessa's and squeezing it caringly.

Tessa's newly harsh expression softened and she felt a bit apologetic herself. She figured she had lashed out a little more aggressive towards her well-meaning friend than she should have. "I'm sorry, Shalena. I know you mean well." She placed her hand on top of Shalena's. "It's just I don't feel like I can really get into figuring out how to trust another person, when I feel like I can't completely trust myself right now."

"I understand, just promise me you won't turn into one of those hermit ladies who lets her career completely consume her life and she totally forgets how to have fun." urged Shalena.

Tessa smiled gently, allowing the sentiment to quietly curve the corners of her lips. "I promise. Now stop worrying about me you mother hen." She said jestingly.

"Okay," reassured her friend.

"Now I have to get home, or I'm not going to get any rest before tomorrow, and I have a feeling it is going to be a very big day." Tessa informed her with a slight sigh as she retrieved her bag that was hanging from the back of the bar stool.

"Alright, honey, I'll see you at home then." Shalena leaned over the bar and placed a small pecking kiss on Tessa's cheek. "Now don't stay up too late, yeah?"

"I promise, I won't." Tessa said as she waved good bye to her friend and began to walk out the door. As she departed through the small entry way to the exit, she could hear the sound of Shalena playfully reprimanding the men around the bar for heckling her about how she behaved with Tessa. This brought a smile to her face, but it did not linger for long as the thoughts of what she was about to throw herself into came flooding into her mind.

Tessa decided to walk the short way home from the bar, to give her a chance to get what fresh air she could in this environment, and clear her head. She knew she had just promised her friend that she wouldn't be up too late, but there was no way she could keep that promise. Especially now, with all of these things swirling around in her mind. She was going to have to buckle down as soon as she got home and get to the bottom of this. For her own peace of mind, she needed to get to the bottom of this and she needed to do it quickly.

CHAPTER 4

Delinquency

—————— • ——————

Bryson was doing his best to stay conscious, as he sat behind the desk in the main office that would be his second home for the next three months. He had most certainly had a rough night the night before, after he finally arrived at his home, following his meeting with his father and brother. He had spent the remainder of the night partially staring at the smoothly painted ceiling of his bedroom, and the other half staring at the glaring blue reflection of his digital alarm clock, in the large glass panes of his bedroom windows. The minutes seemed to crawl by as he laid there, like he was in some sort of hellish limbo awaiting the harrowing day that lay before him. It was all he could do to stay focused through the meeting he had with Mr. Gates at eight o'clock this morning. It was only the first of many that he found he would have to attend that morning, going over the projections for the following quarter. The numbers swirled through his mind like bits of a foreign language, he was doing his dead level best to grasp them as quickly as possible, and he felt he was failing miserably. But he couldn't let anyone else see that, especially if he was going to impress his father enough to give him his financial empire. Bryson could almost feel his shoulders slumping over, and a bend in his back from the weight of the oncoming responsibility. It made him unsure if he even wanted to pursue this task at all. Was it worth it? He found himself pondering that question a lot these days. Particularly, in the last few hours. Was he up for the challenge that had been laid before him? Whether he was or wasn't, he knew that he had to be, for the sake of his relationship with his father.

Bryson had spent so much of his young life doing things that made his father hang his head in shame, and this was the perfect opportunity to change his opinion of his eldest son. He couldn't screw this up, he just couldn't. This was his only chance to make things right, to make his father proud of him before it was too late. Not to mention, a great chance for him to prove that he was more capable a man than his brother. But that was just a bonus and he would enjoy every second of it. For all of his doubting himself, he still found that he was very sure he would get the position of CEO. Like everything else in his life, things had a way of just handing themselves to him, and he felt that even though he was quite fearful, it was probably for nought. Why would this situation be any different?

Bryson stood up for a moment and looked out over the expanse of the city as he let out a breath. His eyes took in the sight of all of the jutting tops of the buildings that glittered in the late morning sunlight. They appeared different to him now than they had the night before. He figured it was because they were all at eye level now instead of just ominously towering over him as they had only a few hours earlier. This made him feel more like the king of this castle than he ever had, now that he was in the corner office. He was now more than a brief visitor, it was his and it was his job to take ownership of it as best he could. Confidence rushed through him, and he brought his hands almost involuntarily to take the lapels of his jacket, as he swelled with pride in his own capabilities.

"Mr. Stafford?" called a female voice from the door behind him, interrupting his mental pep talk.

He turned quickly on the balls of his feet, nearly tripping as the soles of his shoes snagged on the carpet under them. "Yes." He replied, looking up and down the full length of the beautiful woman that was now his secretary. She was a tall, slender woman in a grayish white pinstriped vest and pants, with a powder blue collared blouse underneath. It highlighted all of her features to their best and most delightful advantage, as did her lovely auburn hair and peaches and cream complexion. There was just something about a red head, but she wasn't just any red head. Her hair had dimensions and it made him wonder if it was natural. He would have to wait until later when they were in a more casual setting, before he bothered to ask her. It was things like this that made him enjoy the prospect of getting to throw impromptu office parties.

"There is someone out here who would like to speak with you." The young woman said.

"Oh, okay. Who is it?" Bryson asked nervously straightening his tie and jacket in anticipation of meeting a client.

"It's someone from the first floor, they say they have a matter that needs to be discussed with you and only you." The secretary answered.

"Oh, I see." Bryson calmed down slightly. "Alright, Cherie? It's Cherie, isn't it?"

"Yes, sir." Cherie responded with a delightful toothy smile and quiet chuckle.

"Don't worry, I'll get it eventually. You see, I'm still a bit new to this." Bryson apologized.

"That's okay, sir. Should I send her in?" Cherie asked, motioning to the outer office behind her.

"Yes, yes, go ahead." Bryson replied and watched as Cherie began to open the door a little wider. "Oh, and Cherie…"

"Yes, Mr. Stafford." Cherie said.

"If you could, please, stop calling me Mr. Stafford. Whenever anyone says that I find myself looking around for my father. If we could just do away with the formalities altogether, I think that would make this transition a little easier on me. And, probably you, too." Bryson took a seat on the edge of the front of his desk.

Cherie smiled once again, making Bryson feel like the lights in the room became even brighter as she did so. This was going to be a fun three months, he told himself.

"Alright then, whatever you say. You're the boss." She acquiesced coyly with a slight twinkle in her eyes that made him feel a rush of blood up his legs and into his pelvic area.

"Yes, I am." He replied playfully, as he did his best to cool down before the entrance of his first floor employee. As his secretary departed, he felt a sense of ease pass over him that reassured him he had these next three months in the bag, as long as he dealt with it in the same manner he had always dealt with everything. Fast and loose, always finding the fun in things, and not stressing too much about the small stuff; like formalities. He would make his employees enjoy his reign so much that they would be begging for him to return as their permanent CEO, before his brother's three months had even started.

The door opened once again and Cherie let the young woman pass through the door. He paused for a moment and took in her form as well. She was a young woman of average height, with a petite and attractive frame, she had long dark hair that was imprisoned on the top of her head in a militantly tight bun. He mused to himself what a crime it was that these accountant types felt the need to be so uptight with how they presented themselves. She wore a gray pantsuit that somewhat flattered her body and a dark, navy collared Oxford dress shirt that seemed to tell everyone that she was trustworthy. A very straight laced by the book sort of character, and he got the sudden sense that this meeting was not going to be a pleasant one. But no matter, he was going to turn her serious and stern expression into a smile before the meeting was over. He was sure of it.

"Oh, Cherie." Bryson stopped his secretary as she began to close the door behind the young woman. "Would you do me the kindness of making a reservation for lunch? Oh, you know what? Scratch that, order in for us and that will give us a chance to get better acquainted and you can give me the grand tour of my new floors." He smiled as charmingly as he could manage.

"Yes, sir. No problem. I'll tell them to hold your calls until afterwards. How about that?" Cherie suggested.

"That sounds great, thank you Cherie, you're amazing." Bryson beamed.

"Thank you, sir. I know." Cherie smiled back and slowly closed the door.

The young woman stood there in silence. Bryson was not sure if she was nervous or angry. He thought he had always been a good judge of people's expressions and body language, but she for some reason was a bit of a mystery to him.

"Here, come have a seat." He directed her over to one of the two leather covered chairs that sat in front of his desk. "We're a bit informal around here, now, I guess. I'm Bryson, I'll be your CEO for the next three months." He said in a manner that a waiter would introduce himself. He laughed slightly at his own jesting, but she didn't seem to find the same humor in his words as he did. He extended his hand to shake hers and she took it briefly and awkwardly reciprocating the gesture.

"I'm Tessa Clayton," She introduced herself in a quiet, feminine voice.

"Well, hello Tessa. What has brought you to see me, and only me as my secretary instructed me, this morning?" Bryson asked in his best attempt at a professional tone.

"Well, you see, sir." Tessa pulled the file folder out from under her arm and began to open it. "I received an email to my work hub last night from the third floor and..."

"Oh, that's nothing to worry about. I'm sure things like that happen all the time. You don't have to worry about doing anything about it. I'll just alert them to their mistake. And, I assure you it won't happen again." Bryson interrupted her with a slight clap of his hands that he felt resembled him patting himself on the back for a job well done. One more crisis averted and he could move on to more important things, like having lunch with the lovely Cherie.

Tessa shook her head for a moment as if she was collecting her composure and began to speak again. "I wish it were that simple, Mr. Stafford."

Bryson cringed slightly at her calling him by his surname, and her words stopped him in his tracks as he made his way to the other side of the desk, thinking that their encounter was over. "What else seems to be the issue, Mrs...Miss Clayton?" He looked at her quizzically.

"Miss, I'm not married." Tessa responded.

"Ah," he responded taking a seat in his desk chair. "So what seems to be the problem?"

"The issue is as I was going over these figures last night, it would seem that there is a problem with regards to the contract with The Go-To Construction Guy Company account. They have set up a health and wellness account for the contractors and their security, but the employees have not made any withdrawals for the use of their health and wellness. All withdrawals have reverted back to the company to the amount of approximately a quarter of a million dollars." Tessa explained as she opened the file and came to his side of the desk to give him a better view.

Bryson looked down for a moment at the spreadsheet and mused over the figures for a moment as if he understood what he was looking at. He wasn't quite sure what exactly what he was looking at, but from what he could gather from her words he knew that the outcome of the situation was not a good one. He choked a moment on his reply as he felt the grip of anxiety and fear parch his throat. A sudden attack of itchiness also crawled over his skin like a million tiny spiders, causing him to nearly jump out of his skin, as he almost bounded from his chair. Only to quickly sit down again, unsure of how to react to something like this. Why did he want this job again? He asked himself silently.

"So what do you think, sir? Do you think you can do something about this? What would be our best course of action?" Tessa pelted him with her questions in an almost rapid fire method that seemed to overwhelm him. He nervously rubbed his forehead and the stubble that he could feel peeking through the pores of his chin and jawline. Bryson tried to calm himself with the delightful smell of lavender that had begun to waft into his nostrils. He looked around for a second to see where it was coming from, then realized to his surprise that Miss Clayton's hair must have been the source. This also surprisingly made him happy in this tense moment. With his renewed calm, at the expense of her great shampoo, he felt he could collect his faculties and solve the problem.

"You said you were from first floor, right?" Bryson began by asking. He felt like a man cautiously walking through a field of live land mines praying not to set one off.

"Yes, sir. I am a first floor accounting analyst." Tessa confirmed, standing upright from her leaning position over him. Her face read that she felt she had been standing perhaps too close to him. But he didn't mind at all. She was relatively attractive and he would have preferred a woman to be leaning over him, than one of those smelly overbearing oafs that he usually found presenting these sort of things to him.

"And, you have a department supervisor or something like that, right?" Bryson continued.

"Yes," Tessa confirmed this for him also.

"So, when you told them, if you told them. Did you tell them?" Bryson was doing his best to collect his thoughts as he spoke.

"Yes, I did. I informed Mrs. Davis last night when I discovered this." Tessa informed him.

"And, what, pray tell, did she have to say about it?" Bryson sat back, sinking into the curves of his office chair, and feeling like he finally had some sort of handle on the issue. He began to drum the tips of his fingers against each other, like some sort of maniacal cartoon villain.

Tessa seemed to stand up taller, as if she was becoming slightly irritated by his interrogation. She let out a ragged breath, trying to control her agitation before she spoke. He could see that she was trying to calculate the right thing to say just at that moment. He could only imagine the things that she was contemplating saying before she finally began her exposition.

"She not so informally informed me that this was above my pay grade, and that if I were to tell anyone else about it, it could get around to the rest of the building and I would be unceremoniously fired." Tessa said with a stern sharpness to her words that made him feel he had been sliced. But he recovered as quickly as he could to make light of the grim situation.

"Well, there you have it. Just chalk it up to a screw up on the third floor that will be taken care of by the proper people, and don't worry your pretty little head about it anymore." He responded sitting up in his chair and beginning to issue her towards the door. Bryson was ready for this unpleasant situation to be over as quickly as possible, so he could move on to what he felt were bigger priorities.

"You'll see, there is nothing to worry about. It will all clear itself up in the end."

Tessa briskly collected her file folder from off the top of the desk with a swift and angry swipe as she began to walk out of the office. Suddenly, she paused in the middle of the carpet and turned back to face him. "You know I thought you would be different than the rest of them. I was told take it to the higher ups, they care more about what's going on in their business, because it affects their bottom line. But I guess I was wrong. You're just like the rest of them, too lazy to deal with all the paperwork that this is going to incur. So you are just happy to leave the running of your company to other people like you, who are content to sit on their hands, and have everything handed to them while other people are left to suffer."

Bryson felt a surge of indignance rise up inside of him. She had mortally wounded his pride. Even though he knew deep down that what she was saying was the absolute truth, he couldn't have anyone believing that about him. Or giving him any more cause to believe such things about himself. He fired back, "Well, this company would run much better if certain individuals, you in particular, would learn their place and stay in their own departments; instead of venturing into matters that...as you said, are above their pay grade. And, if you know what's good for you and want to move into a higher pay grade, you'll stay right where you are with your nose to the grindstone and your eyes out of other people's business."

Bryson experienced a pang of fear as he watched her expression become even more fierce with anger. This could end very badly for him, he could sense it. But he was unsure of what to do next. Perhaps it would just take care of itself, and he was relieved when it seemed to.

Tessa's jaw clinched tight as she fought back the words that he could almost see awaiting on her tongue. He almost shrunk back waiting for the impact, but they never came. She turned and he imagined that if her hair had been down it would have whipped him in the face for sure. His eyes followed her swaying yet erect form as she walked out of the room, slamming the door open as she left. The door swung hard and crashed against the adjacent wall with a hard jarring thud that made him wince. Thankfully, nothing was broken, he thought to himself as he looked at the wall to reassure himself.

Cherie came nearly jogging in on her high heels, their clacking filled the air as she came quickly across the tile of the outer office before her steps were silenced by the softness of the carpet in his office. "Is everything alright, sir?" Cherie asked, a look of concern in her eyes.

Bryson took a sip of water from the glass that sat atop his desk and cleared his throat, trying to make sense of exactly what just happened, and what he was going to do if it got out of hand.

"Sir? Bryson?" Cherie's voice came through again.

Bryson looked up to greet her smiling face with a forced smile of his own. "Um...yes, yes. Everything is fine." He paused for a moment, still unable to get his head around everything. And, who was this woman that thought she could just come in here and talk to him like that, in his own office no less. He shrugged, trying to shake off the odd feeling of being put in his place that he had never experienced before now. Well, at least, not since he was a small child being told he couldn't do something by his father. Bryson would most certainly need to find a cure for this and quickly. He knew he had just the thing for it, he turned his attentions back to the beautiful Miss Cherie; who leaned in the door way smiling at him suggestively. And, he was more than willing to take her suggestions. Clapping his hands together gleefully, he proclaimed, "Who's ready for some lunch?"

C H A P T E R 5

Account Termination

———— • ————

The anger within Tessa had reached its utter boiling point. She felt as if the heat from her indignance had made her entire body red and not just her face. Surely, there was visible steam coming out of her ear canals. She could feel the tightness of her hair loosening on the top of her head. She could sense all of her hackles raising, creating the sensation of pins and needles all over her skin, under her now very scratchy pant suit. She needed to get out of here. It was apparent that this place was like everyone else on the planet, dirty filthy liars, that make you think they can give you the moon but fall very short on delivery. Why was it that things like this always happened to her? Couldn't she just catch a break somewhere, for once in her life?

Tessa stood in the center of the thankfully empty elevator, and waited for the doors to open as it descended from the very top floor. It seemed like it took an eternity to reach its destination, which it did with a slight jolt, before the doors gradually opened before her. She stormed out of the small confining box, nearly bolting out like a thoroughbred race horse that had finally been released from its holding stall. She bee lined it to her desk. She was on a mission, and the end of it included her packing up the entire contents of her desk and leaving this building forever. She never wanted to be bothered with the sight of this place ever again if she could help it. Even in passing, she would avert her eyes, she was sure of it. If she didn't take the time to flip them the occasional bird as she rode past them in a cab. Tessa remarked to herself how that was probably not the most mature train of thought, but right now she was not exactly in the best or calmest states of mind. If she didn't know any better, she would have set the whole place on fire before she left.

Tessa paused for a moment to catch her breath as she began to feel very weak and out of breath from her rage. The world was spinning around her and she was certain of a black out if she wasn't careful. A darkness began to encircle her peripheral vision as the sound of pounding filled her ears. She tried to compose herself as she furiously started to throw the contents of her desk into a box. Looking up, she noticed that no one else on the floor was paying attention to the fact that someone was leaving them to do all of this work alone. It was just as she thought, she was just another number on a sheet. This company did not see people as human beings, and that is why they didn't care about doing the right or the honest thing.

She let out a slight huff of breath as she heaved the now surprisingly heavy box into her cradling arms, and began to march down the middle aisle of the first floor that was no longer her department. Tessa made even more purposeful steps, as she started to walk quicker now that she had reached the lobby. Her vision took on that of a tunnel, and all she saw was red when the sight of the entrance came into view. She knew that once she made it outside into the open air she would be okay. A feeling of tightness gripped at her chest and a surge of pain began to run down her arm. She wondered if this was what her mother had warned her about, that heart attack she was sure she would have before she was twenty-seven. Tessa hoped not. How embarrassing would that be, to have a heart attack over getting angry with your boss?

Weaving her way carefully through the crowd traffic of the lobby, she made her way over to the front desk. Tessa did her best to catch her breath that she felt was slowly failing her, as she went to turn in her name badge. There was a man standing there cheerfully talking to the day receptionist. Tessa could barely understand what they were saying to each other, as the pounding in her ears seemed to get louder, and the darkness returned to her vision like lights that flicker, telling you the power is about to go out. In that moment, she saw a shocked and sympathetic expression cross the young woman's face as soon as she saw Tessa. The tall, slender red headed man turned and took on the same expression while he reached out his hands to catch her. Tessa didn't realize it at first, but she was falling quite rapidly towards the floor and before she knew it, everything went completely black. The voices of those around her resounding far away like something out of a distant dream. "Someone quick, call 911! We need to help her! Just hang in there, dear someone is coming."

When Tessa felt she had finally awoke, she was greeted with the sight of two burly looking paramedics. A wash of embarrassment came over her, as she looked around and realized there was a crowd of people standing around her, on their phones taking pictures and probably videoing this for their Instagram stories. Oh god, that was the last thing she needed to be known for; the most exciting event to happen to them at work this week. Great.

"We need all of you to get back and give this young lady some room." called out one of the paramedics, as he helped her to get to an upright seated position. "Slowly, now. You don't want to get a head rush, that could put you right back where you started. Could you look this way for me?" He put up a gloved index finger and directed her eyes towards it as he shined a small light into them. Tessa watched him nod with satisfaction.

"Alright, let's get you up." The other paramedic said, and the two of them lifted Tessa up by the arms and assisted her onto a bench in the middle of the lobby. They began to ask her questions about her medical history and if they needed to take her to the hospital or call someone for her. All she graciously declined and told them she was fine. From over the paramedics, she heard the somewhat familiar voice of a man calling out to the people in the crowd that was still around them, "Go about your business. There is nothing to see here, have some respect. My god!" He approached Tessa in between the two men wearing uniform. He stood there towering tall above her and she felt she had to sit back just a bit to take in all of him.

"What's the verdict, gentlemen?" asked the mysterious unknown man she now remembered from the splices of memory before she blacked out.

The paramedics stood from their seated positions on their knees. "Well, from the looks of it, she's going to be fine. Her pupils are equal and reactive, and she seems lucid enough for her to refuse treatment." one of them replied.

The man looked at her with a concerned and puzzled glance. "Refuse treatment? Are you sure that's wise, my dear? I mean you took quite a tumble. I did my best to catch you but…"

Tessa waved her hand to stop him. "I'm fine really, and thank you for calling them. But I think I can take it from here, really." She did her best to reassure all of them standing around her.

"Well, I guess you heard the lady. She's alright." Said the red headed man.

"Alright, then. I suppose our work here is done." One of the paramedics began before pausing and turning to Tessa. "If you feel at all like this is going to happen again, or you just change your mind, here is my card. We'll come get you." He assured her as he passed her his small, white business card.

"Thank you, I'll be sure to do that." Tessa replied, even though she had no intention of doing so. She was sure this wasn't going to happen again. Just as long as she could go ahead, collect her things, and get out of here as she had previously planned.

"Well, thank you again guys for your speedy response. We always appreciate everything that you do for this fine city of ours. Be sure to stop by the coffee shop on your way out. Tell them Theo Stafford said to give you a freebie, whatever you want." He shook both their hands and patted their shoulders before they departed.

Tessa tried to stand to her feet before the man turned around. She figured if she could make her exit quickly, she wouldn't have to stop too long for idle chit chat. But she was not fast enough. The man turned to face her, trying to stop her from arising from the bench, but he was unable. So he settled for helping her make sure all of her belongings were safely returned to the box that had been resting on the seat beside her.

"Here, let me help you with that." He offered.

"No that's alright, I think I've got it covered." Tessa assured him.

"It's no problem at all, what's your name, darling?" He asked.

Tessa paused for a moment, what could it hurt? "My name is Tessa, Tessa Clayton." She put out her hand to shake his. He tenderly took her hand in his and placed a small kiss on her knuckles. This practice came off as cheesy to her normally, but for some reason she didn't get that vibe from him at all. It seemed to be full of genuine chivalry, which surprised her nearly into blacking out again.

"I'm Theo Stafford, at your service." He responded with a small bow and slight click of his heels. "What seemed to be the trouble, if you don't mind me asking that is? They're not working you too hard up there, are they? What department do you work in anyway? I can't say I have ever seen you before." His voice was as smooth as velvet and put Tessa at ease. She wondered for a moment if this was the universe's way of closing a door yet opening a window.

"I am...well, was a first floor accounting analyst. I've seen you around though." Tessa answered with a twirl of a loose lock of hair.

"That's a pity, I am sure I would have remembered." Theo said regrettably.

"Well, we never actually met in person. I just observed you walking the floor in passing." Tessa informed him.

"Ah, so you noticed me, did you? Alright, I suppose I shall have to be satisfied with that. Let me carry these things out for you." Theo walked over to the bench and before Tessa could protest he had gathered up the box into his arms and stood there proudly at his accomplishment. She knew that his aim was to buy more time with her, and somehow she found herself not minding that much. Tessa observed that he was a very attractive kind of person and he seemed kind and sincere. These were things she found herself craving the most right now after her harrowing and harsh experiences from earlier in the day.

"Alright, I suppose I can't tell you no, now that you already have the box." She said in a voice of surrender.

"I suppose not," He responded as she began to lead him in the direction of the front entrance that was now her exit.

"I heard you say a moment ago that you were a first floor accounting analyst. What happened to change that? Did they fire you?" Theo asked with a tinge of concern and indignance in his voice. It made Tessa really believe that he would do his best to ensure she got her job back if he could. But frankly, even though she had just now discovered him, she still did not want her position back. Not now, not ever.

"Oh, no, it was nothing like that. I've just decided it was time to move on to better things." Tessa spoke to him as one would a man, telling him to put his sword away. "A situation occurred that I would rather not go into too much detail about and I was made privy to how this company is actually run. Which showed me that I no longer want to be a part of it. At least, not if it is run that way."

"That's too bad, I've only just met you and now you're leaving me." Theo said puckering out his bottom lip like a sad puppy, as he backed his way out of the revolving doors. "If things were to change a little, or a lot, would you possibly come back?" He smiled hopefully, his bright, green eyes lighting up as he looked intently into hers. Tessa felt almost enchanted by his gaze, and was overwhelmed by the desire to blush and giggle like some kind of school girl. Her lips began to curl up on the sides and she tried to restrain herself. But the heat radiating from her face told her she blushed anyway, and there was nothing she could do about it.

"Maybe," she finally allowed, still not completely convinced. "But it would have to go through a major overhaul i'm afraid, before that would happen."

"Well, anything is possible, you know? Especially, when you have the proper tools at your disposal." Theo encouraged.

"So they tell me," Tessa digressed.

They stood there on the side walk in silence for a moment, as if they were the only two people around. When finally, Theo broke the staring contest they seemed to be having, and the silence, "At least, let me call you a company car, or a cab if you prefer. I would hate for all of this to have happened to you today, only for something terrible to occur on your way home."

Tessa debated with herself for a moment, but only for a moment. "If it's not too much trouble, really, you have already done so much. You know, calling the paramedics, carrying my things for me...how could I ask you to do anymore?" She politely protested, not meaning a word of it. For she knew he would see right through it and do exactly what he had planned in the first place.

"Just like that. Really, it's no trouble at all." Theo turned to scan the faces of the driver's that lined the curb outside. When he finally settled on one he called out, "Tom!" The man looked up from his phone and began to walk towards them.

"Yes, sir, Mr. Theo." The man said.

Theo carefully handed him the box of Tessa's things in his arms. "Would you please see that Miss Clayton..."

"Tessa," she corrected him, more to tell him that it was alright for him to call her by her first name. He cast a bright, toothy smile in her direction before he continued.

"Be sure that Miss Tessa, makes it home safely, would you?" He asked Tom.

"Yes, of course, Mr. Theo. You can trust me." Tom replied. "Come on, Miss Tessa, my car is this way."

Theo kissed her hand once again and said, "He's right, you're in very capable hands. He will be sure to get you home promptly and safely."

"I really do appreciate everything you have done today. You didn't have..." Tessa tried to thank him, but he raised his hand to stop her.

"There is no need to thank me, I am just doing what any decent human being should do. At least, one with any common sense or courtesy anyway. Like you would for me, I'm sure." Theo reassured her.

She found that all she could do was nod her response. His courteousness and carriage of himself had her quite flabbergasted, but in the best possible way. Tessa felt herself do something very involuntary and somewhat out of character. She leaned forward and gave him a hug good bye. Pulling away they smiled at one another for a moment more, "I really should be going." Tessa urged reluctantly, almost apologizing to herself as she began to walk away.

"I understand. I really should get back in there myself. Until next time then." Theo said squeezing her hand slightly as she pulled away and began to depart backwards in order to keep looking into his eyes.

"Next time?" She asked with a curious hopefulness in her voice. He only looked on with a smile that told her he was most certainly planning on a next time. And, somehow she couldn't wait to see how that turned out.

By the time Tessa had gotten into the back seat of the behemoth of a black town car waiting for her on the curb, and told the kindly driver her home address, she had all but forgotten what caused her to get so angry in the first place. Well, not everything. She remembered the feeling of her righteous indignance, and her desire to slap the smarmy and condescending look off the face of that little boy who was pretending to be CEO. Tessa also thought about why she would never return to work for Stafford Financial, unless Theo somehow found a way to do as he had promised, and give it a complete overhaul. And somehow, she felt that if anyone could, it would be him.

A smile washed over her face and sent a sensation of warmth and comfort over her body, as she settled more into the back seat of the car and watched the sights fly by her window aimlessly. She took comfort in the confidence that she felt now, as it told her that maybe things would not be so bad after all.

<h1 style="text-align:center">CHAPTER 6</h1>

<h1 style="text-align:center">Fraud Alert</h1>

———— • ————

Bryson had done his best to distract himself from the repercussions the previous events of the day had had on his mind. He felt like a man that had thoroughly been run over and over again, by a very large truck. He could still feel every bone crushing roll of all eighteen wheels, as they tumbled over his ego, leaving him broken and bloody in the street of his mind and emotions. What had he done to deserve life being so tough on him right now? Was this his universal debt that had been building up for a while, and now they were coming to collect it all at one time? He wasn't sure, but he kept recalling the old saying, "When it rains it pours." And, the pressure from his oncoming head ache made him wish that it would hurry up and rain. He couldn't tell if it was the barometric pressure outside from the threatening spring storm that was causing his near migraine strength monstrosity, or if it was the sheer amount of information overload that he had received over the course of the day.

He dragged his now squeaking Dolce loafers down the hall as he walked to his designated elevator. His feet seemed like swollen clown feet in tight shoes. He was certain that he had never done as much walking as he did today in his entire life. Hopefully, this was something that he would not have to become accustomed to as the new CEO. If that were the case he would certainly have to do some new delegation of tasks.

Bryson pressed the down button on the wall and the elevator doors opened very quickly, revealing an empty room. He was thankful for this, at least he would get to ride down in peace. Just when he thought he was completely alone, a hand stopped the doors from shutting all the way and pulled them open again. Bryson was slightly startled by this, then he found himself somewhat put at ease when the doors slid back to show him that it was only his brother Theo.

"Do you mind if I join you?" Theo asked, letting himself in. Pretty much telling Bryson that he didn't really care if he had any objections, he was going to ride down with him anyway.

"No, that's alright with me." Bryson acquiesced, knowing he didn't really have any choice in the matter. He began to silently grumble to himself as he threw subtle glances in Theo's direction. He watched as he stood staring at the doors, smiling to himself, always the same expression of a cat that was so proud of himself for eating the canary, and he didn't care who knew it.

Bryson stood there a moment longer, in the close silence that covered everything like a thick, suffocating wet blanket. His mind continued to scramble over the previous events of the day and the very angry first floor accounting analyst, Tessa. He remembered her name very well. It would be forever stamped in his mind, if only because she was the first person to tell him what kind of a person he was, and she was right. He knew deep down that the situation that she brought to his attention was certainly not a good one, and it could definitely mean their ruin if it was left to fester. And, he would be forever painted as the guy that ruined his father's reputation. This would of course, leave Theo to be seen as the hero riding in on a white horse to save the day, and make him even more the apple of his father's eye. Bryson laughed at how appropriate this was, considering the color of his brother's hair. This also brought another thought into the forefront of his mind. Why was Theo seen as the golden boy anyway? Bryson figured this was most likely because he had more of a mind for the business than he did, he always had. His interests lay in the organization, running the numbers, and making sure everyone was performing at their peak. Maybe, this impromptu ride down to the lobby was an act of serendipity. He really needed advice from someone who knew about how to handle this sort of thing and the only person he could think of right now was his brother. For he surely couldn't go to his father with this now, that would just show him to be the weakling that everyone thought he was. Especially himself. But he needed to find a way to do it in such a way that it was inconspicuous. Suddenly, a light bulb went off in his mind and he was sure this would work without causing any undue attention.

"Hey, you know, I think I'm really beginning to get the hang of this." Bryson proclaimed to Theo in as confident of a voice as he could muster.

Theo tilted his head slightly to acknowledge that he heard him. "That's good," he responded.

Bryson took a deep breath like he was preparing to go under water or rip off a band aid. He knew it would be better to just go ahead and get it over with, get the information he needed, and get out before his brother could notice why he was asking him about it. "I have a bit of a strange situation I would like your opinion on." Bryson began.

Theo paused for a moment looking a little stunned and staring at Bryson like he had five or six heads. "You want my opinion? Who are you and what have you done with my brother?" He chortled behind his teeth.

"I know, I know, it's a little weird. But I'm a little bit stumped..."Bryson began again.

"Well, that's not an unusual condition for you." Theo interrupted.

"Hey," Bryson put his hands up to get his brother to give him closer attention. "This is serious, okay. I heard about something today that had me a little rattled." He stepped back like a frightened little boy and began to shuffle his feet on the carpet of the elevator floor.

"Wow, this really is serious." He heard Theo's voice take on a more concerned tone. "Does this have to do with our company? Do we need to consult father? Because if you need to call in the big guns, there is no shame in admitting that you can't handle something. I mean this is your first time really taking on a task like this. I knew father shouldn't have thrown you to the wolves like..."

"No, no, no! It's nothing like that, I can handle things just fine, for your information. In fact, today was a pretty good day surprisingly." Bryson insisted, sounding more like he was trying to convince himself than his brother. But he couldn't worry about that right now.

"Alright, fair enough, so what is this matter that has you so rattled?" Theo asked cordially.

"Well, while we were in the meeting today someone talked about a situation where it was discovered that there was embezzlement in their company. And, it wasn't just the usual sort of embezzlement where you can fire a few department managers and send them to jail. This is the kind that if it were found out at all, there could be jail time for everyone involved. Even those higher up." Bryson tried to explain as cryptically as he could without giving away too much information that would tell his brother he had just lied to him.

Theo closed his eyes and shook his head as Bryson could tell he was trying to digest all of this broken information. "Okay, so explain yourself. What is this big problem? What were they doing?"

"As far as I know, there was some mention of their company having set up some sort of health and wellness accounts, instead of making everyone have to buy insurance that couldn't afford it. Except, the money that they were taking out of the employee's pay checks was being reverted back into various nondescript parts of the company, rather than being used to pay for the employees benefits. Plus, even though the employees have been told that they can access the money, they haven't seen a cent of it." Bryson clarified, as best he could without giving too much away.

Theo stood there wide eyed and thoughtful for a moment. "There is a company actually doing this now?" Theo's voice took on almost a panicked sound.

"Oh, no, I just heard some of the fellas talking today while we were waiting on Mr. Gates. One of them mentioned something about how someone had done that. I don't think their doing it now." Bryson began to feel like he was in some sort of old fashioned comedy movie, where he was having to feed out a lot slack from a rope, before hanging himself.

"Phew!" Theo wiped phantom sweat from his brow as he began to walk about a little in the cab of the elevator. "Well, as long as no one is doing that now. You know if you were to hear something like that, especially about our competition, you would need to go to the authorities with it. Because if they even suspect that you knew something about one of these other fat cats and you didn't tell them, you'll be the one they nail first, and it will just a be trickle down from there or up. Wherever, they don't care. They are the IRS and they do not play my friend, no sir."

"Oh, I know, I guess that is why it had me so rattled. Because, you see, say something like that were to be brought to one of our attention; here at the company. How would a CEO go about dealing with something like that?" Bryson asked as innocently as he knew how.

The raising of Theo's brow did not give him any comfort, and he began to wonder if he was not as clever as he thought he was. Theo waited for a moment in silent thought, as if he was trying to deliberately cause Bryson to sweat in his own panic. A slight smile came to his eyes and he said, "Well, the proper thing to do in this type of 'hypothetical' situation." Theo made the sign of air quotes next to his face. "Is to conduct a quiet investigation. This way you do not alert those who are creating your problem. Like cancer, if this is caught early enough it can be dealt with in a timely and clean fashion. There is no need for unwanted and unflattering publicity; which not only makes you look bad, but destroys all future trust in the company. Ultimately losing you billions of dollars in potential customers, who will now be running to your competition. That is the worst thing about being in this business, you know?" Theo ended his explanation with a question.

"What's that?" Bryson answered his question with another query of his own.

"Well, once something like this happens to sully the face of a company. No one lets you forget about it. Kind of like father, they keep a record of everything you have done and never let you forget." Theo informed him.

"Oh, I see." Bryson's heart sank deep into his chest and he wondered if there would still be any hope for him to preserve his relationship with his father after this, if it ever got out that is.

"Also, like father, our competition has eyes and ears everywhere around us; watching our every move. Just waiting to report back to him or someone else on how we are running this company, and showing them how they could do it much better." Theo continued to speak, but Bryson became very excited as he saw that the elevator was approaching the ground floor, and he wouldn't have to listen to this utterly terrifying monologue any more.

He let out a reserved sigh of relief and tried to pass it off as a yawn, to tell his brother that he was very tired after his long day of work. Theo stepped off of the elevator first and into the opening that led to the underground parking garage. Bryson thought that he was free of him at last as he watched him walk away, but that of course was too easy. Theo stopped for a moment and turned to face Bryson once more. "This is why I need to urge you, brother of mine, be mindful of those around you. You never know who might be here to watch you and report back to father. Or worse, our competition."

"But isn't that like, corporate espionage, or something? And, that's illegal, they can't do that." Bryson informed his brother.

"Well, so is embezzlement, and people feel like they can do that." Theo countered effectively, shutting Bryson up for a moment. He stood there with his jaw slack, unsure how to recover from the comeback. "So, I would tell your friend, or whoever; they need to deal with this problem quickly and quietly, because it could end disastrously...for everyone involved, and not just the CEO. This is one of those things that can destroy a person's entire life. And, I would hate to see that happen to anyone." Theo looked him dead in the eyes when he said this, and the seriousness of his expression made Bryson wonder if he had caught on to what he was saying. Hopefully not, but he couldn't be sure, for he knew that his brother was much cleverer about matters such as this than he ever was.

Bryson marched purposefully towards the black town car that waited for him in its designated parking spot. He was happy to see Tom there waiting for him. They made the usual ride home small talk as his mind wandered in an out of the conversation; while he wracked his brain about who he could possibly hire to get him out of this situation, or at least look into it without alerting his father. He needed someone honest and honorable that he could trust. Just when he thought he had run out of hope, serendipity struck again, and Tom began to talk about someone he gave a ride home to earlier that afternoon. He said she was a young lady who had decided to quit her job because the company had turned out to be a dishonest den of thieves, and she couldn't justify being a part of something like that.

A rush of hope and happiness ran through Bryson giving him a new energy and bringing light to his eyes. By George, he had it! He began to feel a plan formulating in his head, he didn't quite have all the answers to his problem yet, but he knew where he could find the key. And, her name was, Tessa Clayton.

CHAPTER 7

Account Reinstatement

·

The lines of words began to blur into squiggly lines on the screen before her, as Tessa tried to focus her sleep deprived eyes enough to read the rest of the job postings on the page. She had been up all night once again, and she was still determined to stay up another whole day if that was what it took for her to find a job.

She decided to stop for a moment and take a breather, if only to get a refill on her coffee, before getting back to the drudgery of the online help wanted ads. She had done everything she knew how to do, she had watched every online video on how to spruce up your resume, and even created several accounts on various job hunting sites. The only thing that got her was a lot of spam emails about how she needed to get the warranty checked on the car she no longer owned, or asking her what kind of dentures or adult undergarments for bladder incontinence she needed to make her life easier. Shalena and she had had a big laugh about that one last night, when she was nearly delirious from having been up for the last several nights. She knew that Shalena had told her not to worry that she would be able to handle the rent on her own until Tessa could find another job, but she just couldn't justify doing that to her. It made her feel like she would be mooching off of her somehow, and there was no way she was going to be put in a position where she felt that way. Even if the person had the best possible intentions in the world. She just couldn't do it. So this is where this obsession had landed her, standing in front of the coffee pot, waiting for it to brew for the longest time, before realizing she was so tired she had forgotten to press the on button. Finally, she rectified the situation and the nectar of the gods started to flow from the little spout on the brewer, to her great delight. Tessa figured she was probably reacting a little more giddy than she should have over something so trivial. But it really was the small things in life that she had to find joy in right now, after everything had gone so wrong for her recently. It had truly been a rough last couple of years.

Just then, there was a knock at the door. Tessa paused for a moment wondering who it could be at this time in the morning. She was sure it couldn't be one of her neighbors at a time like this, when the sun was barely up, unless it was some kind of an emergency. And, as far as she was aware neither she nor Shalena were expecting any packages. So it was probably not the mail man. But then again, it could be. Sometimes they did get them confused with one of their neighbors apartments. Yet another thing that she was having to become accustomed to, now that she was living in such a big city where everyone was piled in on top of each other like sardines.

Tessa tried as she might not to trip over her own bare feet as she stumbled sleeplessly to the door. Her head spun with delirium as she tried to collect herself as best she could before answering it. She could only imagine how much of a wreck she appeared to be, with her disheveled hair and shiny make-up absent face. Thankfully, she had remembered to continue to put on deodorant and brush her teeth, even if she couldn't recall the last time she showered.

Tessa reached out a trembling hand to open the door. It was not for fear that she was shaking, her muscles had become weakened by her current diet of caffeine and lack of sleep. These were the only compromises she had found herself willing to make to further her career, which seemed to currently be going nowhere at the moment. She whipped the door open quickly before thinking about looking in the peep hole first. When she beheld the individual that stood waiting for her on the other side of the door, she wished that she had and told them to go away. For there stood Bryson Stafford, in all of his GQ ready business casual glory. Tessa felt suddenly that she was terribly under dressed for the occasion. But she didn't really care right now, all she wanted to do was slam the door in his face and fall in a clump in the floor. Maybe, she would be the person to champion human hibernation as a thing. This sounded like a really good idea right about then.

"I know I am probably the last person you want to see right now," Bryson began as Tessa tried to close the door in his face. He put out his hand to stop it and forced it back open.

"That dear, sir, is the understatement of the century. Congratulations, but I am afraid I am all out of the cookie prizes that come with that particular award." Tessa remarked.

"Are you drunk?" Bryson asked, with a slight look of disgust on his face as his eyes scanned her up and down.

"No, I am sleep deprived. They say it's more dangerous, all I know is, it's not as fun." Tessa responded.

"Why are you sleep deprived?" Bryson queried, looking a little confused as he entered the apartment.

Tessa wasn't really sure why she was letting him in, but she didn't have much choice now. He was already past the threshold. "Oh, maybe because of some asshole who told me I needed to mind my own business instead of do the right thing. So I had no other recourse but to leave, and now I am spending all of my time trying to find another job."

"Oh," Bryson replied, sheepishly putting his hands in his pockets and scuffing his feet uncomfortably on the shag rug in the living room.

"So, did you just come here to throw that in my face, or what? 'Cause if you're here to offer me my job back, I'm going to have to answer that with a big fat, no. I think you can understand." She crossed her arms in front of her chest as a last stitch way to try and hold herself in an upright position, even though she wasn't completely certain that it would do the trick, but it seemed to be. So she was satisfied for now. Not to mention, it gave further fuel to the appearance of her attitude, she felt.

"But that's just the thing, I need you to come back. You see, you're the only one that can help me right now. And, I'm desperate." Bryson began to plead with her.

"Oh, okay, yeah right, try again. Why would you, the CEO of Stafford Financial, need the help of poor little first floor accounting analyst like me?" Tessa stopped him in his tracks. "Besides, what makes you think I am going to come back because you're desperate? Just because you beg me to come back, does not mean that I will." She said as sternly as she could without slurring her speech.

"I know I need to offer you more than just my cries for help, and I can give you those things. I am willing to agree to whatever terms you set at this point." Bryson stated. Tessa could sense the sincerity in his words. She saw in his eyes that he was a man who was willing to do anything to save himself right now, and he honestly felt that she was the only one that could do it.

"Keep talking," she waved her hand in a circular wheel like motion for him to continue his explanation, and hopefully his oncoming apology.

"Can I be frank with you?" Bryson asked.

"I would prefer it," Tessa replied.

"Alright, so here it goes." He let out a breath as he sat down on the arm rest of the couch, across from where she was making an effort to stay standing in an upright position. "My father has cooked up this plan to where he has decided to allow my brother and I run the company for an entire quarter, respectively, on a trial basis. He is using this as a way to see which one of us is fit to run the company after he is no longer able to. Do you follow me?"

"It's pretty simple, but I'll try to keep up." She countered.

Bryson smiled nervously, "So, I need your help, since you seem to be the only one concerned with actually dealing with this situation before it gets too out of hand. And, you seem to be the only person I know of that actually understands what's going on. This is why I decided to come to you for help, because I know that I can't trust anyone else at the company right now to be honest enough to sort out who I should turn in to the authorities, and who I shouldn't."

"Why can't you just go to your father with this? Doesn't he have, like, auditors or something that can take care of this without a whole lot of muss or fuss?" Tessa asked a little puzzled, her brain was hurting.

"Well, you see, that's just the thing. I don't want to do that because I am afraid that something this big, if I were to go to him with it, it would only serve to show him how incapable I am to deal with in house company problems. And, I just can't afford to do that. I can't." He punctuated his words in such a firm and passionate manner that Tessa got the impression there was something that lay at the heart of his desires which he was unwilling to share with her. But, she also got the feeling that it had more to do with his relationship with his father, rather than anything to do with how he was running the firm. Tessa began to pace back and forth as she ran over all the pros and cons of the situation in her muddled mind. Finally, she reached a decision after much debate with herself.

"Alright, I'll do it." Tessa stated.

"You will?! Oh that's great!" Bryson jumped up from his seated position and moved forward, almost as if he was ready to hug her. Tessa backed away from him swiftly and put up her hand. She needed to make some things clear first before he could celebrate.

"But," she extended her index finger nearly in his face. "I need to lay some ground rules first." She stated firmly.

"Yes, yes, of course." Bryson sat back down preparing himself for her demands.

"I am going to need access to everything." She began.

"Of course, done. Anything you need." He acquiesced with a fervent nod of his head.

"Second, I am going to need you to understand that these sort of things tend to get very messy. They usually have been going on for quite some time, and you will find yourself finding things out about people you thought were completely different, and incapable of doing things like this. So no matter who turns out to be in on this, I am going to need you to promise that there will be no more of this telling me to mind my own business and sweeping things under the rug, bullshit." Tessa wagged her finger at him once again.

"I promise, no more sweeping things under the rug or telling you to mind your own business." Bryson crossed his heart and held his palm in the air as a sign that he swore to do exactly as she said. "So, do we shake on it? Or what?" He asked looking a little bit at loss for what to do, but relieved at the same time.

"Yeah, we can shake on it. Understand this handshake is as binding as a contract, so anything deviating from the terms that have been laid down here. This contract is considered null and void." Tessa informed him.

Bryson extended his hand as he got up once again. "Yes, of course, I understand."

Tessa took his hand and pulled him in closer to her with a quick jerk of her arm. His expression took on a look of surprise at the strength of her tiny body.

"You see, I don't think you do." Tessa said.

"What do you mean?" His gaze alternated between her hand that still firmly gripped his and the fierce glint in her eyes.

"What I mean is, you do anything that I even suspect to be dishonest, and I will consider this contract invalid. Meaning, that I will take all of this to your father myself. Even what was said here today, understand? Do we still have a deal?" Tessa stared deeply into his striking blue eyes. She had never noticed how beautiful they were before. But then again, at the time that she met him, she wasn't really concerned with his appearance. She figured it must be the sleep deprivation high her mind was currently on, that made her stare at them so intently now. Whatever it was, for some reason she just couldn't help herself.

"You have a deal," Bryson confirmed, the deepness of his voice pulling her out of the hypnotizing pull of his oceanic eyes.

"Alright, so when do we get started?" Tessa asked as Bryson made his way to the door.

"Well, first things first, you should probably get some sleep before you fall over. I guess I will see you sometime tomorrow night after everyone is gone." Bryson answered, opening the door for his own exit.

"Right," Tessa had nearly forgotten she most likely needed to sleep before jumping into this. "This is something that needs to be handled with the utmost discretion."

“You got it,” Bryson stated, saluting her with his index finger. “So tomorrow night, then.”

“Tomorrow night,” she reciprocated the salute as he closed the door behind him and departed.

Tessa threw her arms up in the air and let out a howl, feeling the intense glee of having a job again rush over her. She thought about walking to her bedroom to fall asleep in her own bed, but the couch was in closer proximity, and it looked comfy enough for her to camp out on for now. She stumbled her way over, feeling like if she were to enter a contest for people doing their best impression of the undead, she would most likely win grand prize. She threw herself down like a sack of potatoes onto the cushions of the well-worn couch, and quickly fell asleep.

C H A P T E R 8

Appraisal

———— • ————

Over the next several weeks, Tessa found that the Stafford Financial Group had once again become her second home. In all reality, she was spending so much time there now, her studio apartment had become more like a second home, rather than her primary. But she didn't mind, she was finally making good money again, as well as the bonus of getting to do what she loved most in the world while she was doing it.

When they began, it was obvious that Bryson had no clue what he was doing, and she wondered to herself why his father had even decided to make him CEO in the first place. Because, in spite of his supposedly extensive college education in the field of business and finance, he had not retained any of the information necessary to run a business like this. But to her surprise and delight, she turned out to be a pretty good teacher and he seemed to be catching on quickly.

Now that they had begun to spend so much time together, there was yet another thing that Tessa started to notice about Bryson and also herself. She wasn't sure if it was down to the shared excitement of his making of leaps and bounds, or if it was the fact this event had so unceremoniously thrust them into each other's paths, but she found herself able to begin to let her guard down with him. Maybe even trust him a little. And, she felt that he was starting to do the same with her. In many ways, she found herself becoming afraid of the fact that she was beginning to look forward to the time spent together. Is this what it felt like to develop a true friendship with someone? She wondered to herself. Tessa found she had to think of it as a way to start over with how she viewed her relationships with men. Life had finally handed her a way to build a healthy friendship with someone, so much so that she could eventually move on to possibly having a healthy romantic relationship with someone. But it would most likely not be Bryson, she told herself. He was still too much of a wild, unpredictable, playboy type. Nowhere near stable enough in mind or maturity for Tessa. She found herself becoming annoyed a lot of the time at the fact that he would tend to become whiny at the prospect of working long hard hours. But they were getting through it, somehow. The limit of her aspirations right at this very moment was to solve this mystery for him and somehow move on from here with her sanity intact. If that was even possible, she hoped.

Bryson sat back in his black leather office chair with his legs crossed, propping them up on what was once his father's desk. He was becoming more and more confident every night that it would certainly be his, and he was grateful to the one he knew was giving him this gift. He mused to himself about how remarkable of a woman Tessa truly was. She had turned out to be someone that he had started to envy in a way. He knew this was because of her tenacious can-do attitude and incredible work ethic that he had never taken the time to cultivate or possess. And now, he wished that he had as he watched her even now; while she vigorously began to wipe all of the figures and synergistic circles she had drawn on the white, dry, erase board she had brought into the office. Was it wrong of him to think about her like some kind of sexy school teacher during their time together? Probably so, but he found himself completely unable to help himself. There was just something about her that he was beginning to find desperately attractive. He was now like a moth that was becoming helplessly drawn to the light of her bright, burning flame of confidence and intelligence, and he couldn't explain it.

Bryson thought to himself about how he had never been the kind of a man to pursue a woman for her intellect ever before. Put him in a room with a bunch of leggy, super model types who cared way too much about their bodies, and what they were or weren't eating, and he was good for a while. He didn't have to worry about anyone making him look foolish because they were all far below him in intelligence. Which if he were to be completely honest with himself, they wouldn't have to go too far down on the rung of mentality to do so. Especially when he compared himself to people like his father and his brother, or even Tessa herself. There was nothing impressive about the things that he stored in the file cabinets of his mind, as she called them. He recalled it as one of the many things that she had taught him over the last few weeks they had spent together. Even though this didn't really have anything to do with solving his problem, it solved a host of others by teaching him how to organize his thoughts in a more productive manner, and he found that he was grateful to her for that as well. It had opened up a whole new world for him to be able to participate more like the leader of a company in the board room, and even at home when he was alone. He was truly making the transition to becoming a captain of industry, someone responsible and capable that his father could be proud of, and this he desired more than anything in the world.

    This experience with her had also been very refreshing for him, because she was obviously a woman who was definitely not interested in hopping into bed with him or anyone for that matter. Normally, he viewed women like this as if there was something wrong with them, and that was why they were not pursuing a relationship with anyone. But as time had gone on, he had come to realize that her reasoning was because she was focused on getting her life together and making something of herself. Transforming herself into someone that could do just fine with or without a man in her life. This was a healthy kind of emotional caliber that he wanted, and he hoped that if they could spend more time together, eventually this incredible essence of hers would rub off on him. Deep down in the secret place of his heart, he hoped that he could eventually somehow deviate her focus, just enough to show her that he was the man she could be okay with having in her life. If that is what she wanted, because he knew now this was something he definitely wanted.

Bryson had begun to notice that he was becoming something resembling giddy, whenever he thought about the idea of them spending time together. Getting to ride in the car with her on the way home, letting his hand linger on a file just long enough for her to have to touch his skin with hers, and standing close enough to smell the intoxicating scent of whatever she happened to be wearing at the time. At one point, he remarked about the fact that she smelled very pleasant one evening. He asked her what it was, for it was nothing he had ever had the pleasure of smelling before and she very plainly told him that she wasn't wearing anything at all. He nearly fell out of his chair with surprise and near delight at discovering this. He felt a bit silly now that he thought back on it, but he also told himself that this was something…nay, someone that he needed in his life desperately. Every sinew of his body ached with desire for her now. He could feel his heart rate getting faster, his breath shorter, and his palms become sweaty. His words would begin to catch in his throat and he would find that he had great anxiety when he tried to express his thoughts to her. She had completely and utterly bewitched him, and turned him into some sort of blathering idiot every time he was around her. All he was left capable of doing was to sit there and stare at her with a goofy grin on his face. He wondered if she noticed, probably so, women knew these things, but she had not bothered to show any sign that she felt the same way. Could it be that she didn't feel the same as he? He thought to his horror. Or that she just didn't know that he even existed on her radar in that fashion? Bryson mused to his even greater terror. He told himself that deep down there was no way that he could ever deserve a woman like her in the first place, and he would be doomed to spend the rest of his life pursuing bimbos and cheap knock offs of Tessa. Hopping from marriage to marriage, always wishing that he had caught the one that would ultimately get away and find her happily ever after, with someone far more deserving than he.

This put him in a bit of a somber mood by the end of their work night, and he found himself sluggishly and reluctantly helping her gather her files from the desk. She smiled at him with the blinding brilliance of light that she seemed to carry around with her everywhere she went. Tessa was the reason all of the 80's songs that he was so accustomed to putting on his playlist made sense. The song lyrics danced through his head, "every little thing she does is magic, every little thing just turns me on, even though my life before was tragic, now I know my life with her goes on". It overlapped, drowning out the sound of her words as she spoke to him, but all he could hear was the music, and he knew in his heart that the only way for his life to truly go on, was with her and no one else.

CHAPTER 9

Opening Deposit

—————— • ——————

It had gotten late and Bryson and Tessa were very work weary from their long day of mental exertion. Tessa let out a tired sigh as she started to wipe everything off of the erase board that she had set up in Bryson's office, as was her customary nightly routine at the end of their sessions. Once she had completed this task, she quickly turned to make sure she had gathered up all of the papers and various documents from his desk. She felt the warmth of his body, and smelled the pleasantness of his sandalwood cologne as he stood in close proximity to her, helping her to collect everything and put it into a neat, liftable stack. Tessa stood upright for a moment and stretched, groaning as she felt all of the muscles in her back release their various pockets of trapped air. They sounded like someone popping a bag of ready pop in a microwave. She thought to herself about how she really needed to invest in a good chiropractor and get an adjustment. But she would worry about that after taking care of the situation here. For once in her life, she seemed to have all of her priorities in order, she thought. All except one perhaps.

She raised her hand to the back of her head, and had begun to remove the ink pen she had turned into a makeshift hair stick to pull her hair into a messy bun, when suddenly, it became snagged on a lock of her long dark brown hair, and she couldn't seem to dislodge it without a fight. Tessa backed up and turned away, a little embarrassed at the predicament in which she now found herself. She couldn't let him notice her like this, and she tried even harder to remove it. "Oh, come on. How is it I was able to get you in there so easily, but you won't come out?!" She whispered hoarsely to herself under her breath. Then, she felt the warm soft touch of a hand on hers, calming her fiercely fidgeting fingers.

"Hey, slow down. I got it." Bryson's voice travelled like honey into her ears, covering her frantic state with an ocean of peace. She let down her hands and found herself enjoying the touch of his fingers in her long hair, as he deftly untangled the strands from their place behind the clip. The sensation of icy hot tendrils flowing down the nerves of the back of her neck, was over sooner than she wanted it to be when he had finally freed her hair from its pen prison.

"There, all better." Bryson said, reaching his strong tanned arm around her shoulder and presenting the offending ink pen to her. She leaned back slightly into him as she slowly removed it from his long able fingers.

"Oh, thank you. I wasn't sure I was ever going to get that out of there again." Tessa quipped, she felt awkwardly. The feelings that ran over her made her feel like a fool with nothing appropriate to say.

He smiled warmly in her direction, his gaze slowly colliding with hers, and lingering there for a while. She was soon awash in the deep striking blue of his Aquarian eyes, and she felt she would never escape. She would not have fought her fate even if she were indeed doomed to drown in them. What was this feeling? She asked herself. Had she completely lost her mind? Tessa closed her eyes and shook her head as if trying to break some kind of hypnotic spell. She needed to focus on the priority at hand, and right now that meant getting all of this cleaned up and returning home to her bed for a much deserved night's rest.

Tessa briskly walked over to the desk, gathered up the stack of files into her arms and began to walk away in the direction of the office door, leaving him behind. But he quickly followed her, his long legs having no trouble to fall into step with hers. She smiled up at him as he opened the door for her and stepped through as swiftly as she was able, again trying to walk away from him as fast as she could. She couldn't risk pursuing the feelings she was now feeling for him. This was dangerous, and if she allowed herself to dwell on them much longer, she was certain that things would end up exactly where neither of them needed to be. As much as she found herself desiring a result that concluded in them waking up in the same bed, she knew it was not for the best for either of them right now.

Tessa tried to push all thoughts of his muscled, tan, arms which she found herself all too often admiring late at night as they worked together. Hoping a little too much that he would feel a bit warm and need to roll up the sleeves of his button up shirt. He always wore such good colors for his skin. Never had she known a man to be able to pull off the color purple like he could. It was what he was wearing tonight, and she found that it was most certainly her favorite of all the shirts in his wardrobe. What was she doing? She asked herself once more. Only girlfriend's concern themselves with things like a favorite piece of a man's wardrobe or the smell of their cologne, the way that their shoulders were delightfully broad enough for you to imagine yourself lying under him and running your fingers over them, before caressing the rest of the rippling muscles of his back. She began to feel herself becoming a bit warm, and she was sure that her skin was turning pink from the heat. She really needed to stop this, as she had told herself before she was traveling into dangerous territory, and needed to be very cautious of her next actions.

Tessa frantically pressed the down button of the elevator as she heard the foot falls of Bryson's loafer shod feet close in behind her. She felt like someone trying to throw off their trail from someone in hot pursuit, but she was trying to trying to throw him off for a completely different reason. For it was not he that she was afraid of, it was herself and what she might allow herself to do if she found herself getting too close to him.

"Where's the fire?" joked Bryson as he fell in beside her while she waited for the doors to open. It felt like they were taking forever.

"Oh, nowhere. I just really want to get home." Tessa tried to politely tell him she didn't want to spend any more time around him right now. The doors finally opened, Tessa stepped in quickly and Bryson followed suit. They stood there in silence listening to the elevator music for a while. Tessa did her best to keep her eyes to herself, trying as hard as she might to think about anything else but him and his body, or how great he smelled. This was very difficult for her with the two of them standing in this small, confining box that seemed to be getting smaller and smaller by the minute. She could feel herself beginning to blush as the glare of his striking eyes seemed to peer into her soul, from out of her peripherals. The touch of their gaze was maddening like the soft caressing of his fingers in her hair only a few moments ago.

Tessa was grateful for the swiftness of the elevator reaching the ground floor parking garage. The doors slid open with a whirr and a thud as they forcefully hit the inside of the back wall, bringing a jarring halt to Tessa's thoughts for which she was also grateful. She marched briskly from the inside of the elevator, feeling the hope that perhaps she would finally escape him, at least for tonight. But she was wrong. The sound of his graceful but heavy, manly, jogging steps followed behind her in a closeness that made her quicken her pace. She was not really certain what for now, for she was sure that she could no longer outrun him, and might as well just accept whatever fate the universe had in store for her tonight, and possibly the nights to come after. Tessa slowly turned to face him as she was stopped by the body of the town car in front of her. There was nowhere else for her to run without making it look like she was purposefully trying to avoid him.

Bryson put out his hand and rested it on the car, as if he was trying to stop her from opening the door leading to the back passenger seat. He caught his breath and Tessa realized that he had truly been running to catch up with her. This told her that the feelings she had begun to detect in herself not only belonged to her, but to him as well. The mingling of their hearts communicating with each other had given strength to the power of their...dare she say it...love?

"Hey, would you like to go get some dinner, or something?" Bryson asked in an almost pleading tone of voice.

Tessa heard the fog horn alarm bells go off in her head and she knew that if she didn't refuse now, she would never get away. "Oh, I would, but I'm really tired and I need to get home. Maybe, some other time." She pleaded, knowing she really meant most likely the tenth of never.

"Well, I mean, I'm sure you're pretty hungry too after everything we just did in there. You can really work up an appetite doing all of that...math." Bryson made a goofy, yucky face, which brought a bit of a smile to hers and she chuckled softly at his antics that she now found to be cute, instead of annoying as before.

"No, I really should be going. Besides, I don't look like someone that needs to be going out right now." Tessa politely protested, moving her hand slowly towards the door handle of the car door behind her back.

"It doesn't have to be anywhere fancy, nowhere like that would probably be open this time of night anyway. How about pizza? You like pizza don't you? I would have to think you were a little weirder than I already do if I found out you live in New York and you don't like pizza." He quipped as he continued to urgently try to convince her to eat with him.

"Oh, really? You think I'm weird, huh?" Tessa smiled as she asked, and the blush returned to her cheeks as she tried to stop herself from flirting, but it was to no avail. Her desire for him washed over her like the tides of the sea in his eyes as they drew her in further, and she felt her body draw closer to his. Oh, how she could see him, in her mind's eye, pressing her against the side of the car right now. The full weight of his taut, muscled form crashing into her slender, supple frame and his warm, full, welcoming lips placing a passionate kiss on her moist, awaiting mouth. She had to stop this or she was certain that it would happen and she would be the instigator. Tessa urged herself to speak, like someone desperately trying to wake themselves from a fevered dream. "Oh, alright, I'll get a pizza with you. What could that hurt, right? A little dinner amongst, friends?" She was setting the ground rules more for herself than she was him.

Bryson's expression seemed unfazed by her utterance of the word "friends".

"Yeah, just a simple no strings attached, ordinary pizza." Bryson replied, reaching behind her and beginning to open the car door for her. The brush of his hand on the small of her back caused her to almost allow a gasp to escape, but she restrained herself. She couldn't risk letting him know the war that was raging even now between her mind and body.

"Okay," she agreed.

He opened the door and let her enter the car first before sliding in beside her on the seat. Tessa thought about how he was sitting a lot closer tonight than he usually had. Everything began to feel like she had done all of this before, as if this was something they did all the time. A sudden sense that this felt right hit her like a ton of bricks and it thoroughly frightened her, but she couldn't let herself show it. There was a feeling that he felt the same way as well, but she couldn't understand why she was more afraid than he. Perhaps he had not been burned as she had so many times before, and that is why it was easier for him to just slide in and enjoy how right and peaceful this seemed.

It wasn't long before Bryson told Tom to pull over and let them out so they could walk. The spring night air brushed against her face and refreshed her mind and spirit as she felt it cooling her down. What she needed was a tall glass of ice water, or a sudden downpour of cold rain. She needed to calm down and slow her roll before she found herself doing something stupid. Tessa took a deep breath as she watched Bryson walk to the open window of the walk up pizza vendor. She told herself to just live in the moment and take each moment as it came. There was nothing to fear here, she was a level headed woman with clear priorities, and winding up in bed with him tonight was not one of them. She was sure he would find what she was thinking to be silly and perhaps even embarrassing if he were to find out. So she did her best to keep any signs of her underlying intentions to herself. This was just as he said, two friends getting an ordinary no strings attached slice of pizza after work, nothing more.

They sat there on the bench on the side walk near to the pizza vendor. Tessa felt a little safer from herself as they shared a few laughs and some idle chit chat. She just concentrated on the flavor of the fresh pie in her hand and the coolness of the night rather than reading too much into his longing glances and his offhand remarks, that triggered skips of her heart. She told herself she would just use this time as an opportunity to practice having a healthy friendship with a man, instead of running straight in to pursuing the romantic side of it.

"So have you lived in New York all of your life?" Tessa asked him, continuing to make small talk.

"Yes, even though, my family is not originally from here. I am a native though." Bryson replied, wiping his mouth between bites of pizza. "What about you, Tessa? Have you been a New Yorker all your life?"

"Yes, pretty much. But my family moved us to upstate New York pretty early on, because they didn't like the hustle and bustle of the big city life when it came to raising their children." Tessa responded.

"Ah, I see. You say children. Does that mean you have siblings?" Bryson queried innocently, but Tessa felt a pang of pain and guilt consume her heart like the stab of an icy dagger, and she quickly had to take a drink of her soda to fight back the tears that threatened to pour from her eyes. She coughed slightly to clear the lump from her throat before she answered a lot quieter and more weakly than she anticipated or wanted to.

"Um...yes, I...I had a brother, Geoffrey." Tessa replied hoping that he wouldn't pursue this line of questioning too far.

"Oh, yeah? I have a brother, Theo. He's younger than me, even though he likes to pretend he's older and knows more than I do. Is your brother like that? Or are you pretty close?" Bryson prodded.

"I guess you could say we were pretty close. He had every right though to act like he knew more than me, because he was my older brother after all." Tessa clarified.

"Was?" Bryson's voice took on a more serious and surprised tone.

"Yeah, I don't really like to talk about it. But I suppose I should sometime, at least to somebody other than the family." Tessa exposited.

"It's good to get it out in the open every once in a while, it shows you how much you've healed or you haven't." Bryson added.

This statement took Tessa aback a bit. "You sound like a man who has lost someone as well." Tessa felt she was prying now.

"Yeah, when we were very young. My mother had decided take our baby brother, Clive, to see her mother because she hadn't had a chance to see him yet. We were going to go with her, but my father had something else planned for us to do instead. I can't remember exactly, but I'm sure it wasn't too important. They were supposed to arrive home that evening and they never arrived." Tessa's mind flashed with memories of how they learned of her brother's death in the same way, and she felt a kindred grief that brought her closer to Bryson as he spoke.

"My father received the call the next morning that they had gotten into an accident the night before, and their bodies were so badly ravaged by the wreck, it took them until the next morning to figure out who they were." Bryson finished, his voice trailing off as he began to stare off into the middle distance. Tessa wasn't sure if it was because he was trying to forget the thought of the terrible tragedy or if he was wallowing in the pain of his shattered family.

"That's pretty rough, I'm so sorry, Bryson. I had no idea." Tessa sympathized, her own grief for her broken family coming through in her voice.

"Don't be sorry, not a lot of people know anyway. It's not like it's something I go around advertising. Besides, father doesn't like to talk about it. I think it is because somehow he knew that Clive would probably have out done all of us when it came to taking over the business. And he wouldn't have even bothered with this silly trial period and just handed everything over to him." Bryson surmised, tossing the Styrofoam cup full of ice gruffly into the aluminum public trash can a few yards away from him on the side walk.

"No, don't say that. You don't know that at all." Tessa scolded him, scooting in closer to him on the bench. The side of her bare leg grazing his from under her skirt. "You are just as capable as either one of your brother's, dead or alive. And, your father, too."

Bryson looked at her with a sense of incredulous pride and happiness, as well as relief. "You really think so?" He asked.

"I do," Tessa placed a reassuring hand on his back and rubbed it gently.

A strange, almost magical feeling came over the both of them, and the reflection of the street lights seemed to dance like little fairies in his dark hair, and from his skin. Tessa could feel a nearly magnetic pull drawing her closer to him. There was no escaping for her now and she could do nothing but allow herself to surrender to the magic of the moment.

Bryson's soft, warm welcoming lips pressed up against hers, gently at first. Before Tessa could pull away or control herself, she was fervently and hungrily returning his kisses. The moist, beckoning chasm of his mouth opened compliantly, and his firm tongue slid over hers with a deftness and ability she had never experienced from anyone she had ever kissed before.

The passion raged within her, threatening to reach a boiling point, she couldn't allow herself to fall any further, as the sensations quickly began to transform into a great fear that also began to consume her. Tessa tore herself away violently and bolted from the bench, running across the busy street, and nearly being hit by an oncoming cab in the process. The sound of Bryson's shocked and surprised voice called after her in the growing distance between him. She wasn't really sure where she was running to, she just knew she needed to run as far away from him and her feelings as quickly as her legs could carry her. And she did just that, fading into the night, vowing not to look back...at least until tomorrow.

CHAPTER 10

Bullish

———— • ————

The next morning Tessa was a complete and muddled mess in her mind. How could she have allowed herself to fall that far last night? Was it a mixture of the bond she had built with him over the last few weeks, and the grief they now had in common? That must be it, she told herself. Surely, it could be nothing more than that. But somehow she couldn't rationalize it enough within herself for it to fit into that category. She had run over the events that led to that crucial point last night so many times in her mind. Just like any other equation, it all came out to one simple answer. Bryson was the one for her and she need not have any other. In spite of the screaming voices of her previous pains from her last failed relationships, she found herself somehow able to quiet them with the thought of allowing Bryson into her life. There was no other solution to the problem she felt within herself. He was the other half of her empty equation, and she needed to tell him that before it was too late.

Tessa quickly dressed for work and departed the apartment for the Stafford Financial building on Wall Street, with a speed that she was sure would make it into some kind of record book. Her desire to be at his side seemed to give wings to her feet, carrying her over the busy and bustling crowded city streets she was so familiar with by now. Today however, she took no notice of all of the other offensive things that usually assaulted her sight and other senses, as she made her way to the all too familiar sanctuary. It was truly now her sanctuary, for her harbor of calm dwelt there, and his name was Bryson Stafford.

She arrived at the entrance of the building in record time. Making her way strategically and clandestinely, she found herself on the back elevator that led directly to the top offices. The ride was slower and more agonizing than she had ever remembered it being before now. She figured it was because she was so very anxious to see him again, and to apologize for running away last night. Hopefully, it wasn't too late. She desired now more than ever to hold him in her arms and feel his lips on hers once again. And, she would be sure to savor every second of it and never allow herself to pull away ever again.

The doors pulled open but not fast enough for Tessa, and she slid through the narrow space between them before they could fully open. She made the slight turn and ran down the hallway to Bryson's office, not stopping to take notice of his secretary who stood to stop her from going in. She quickly threw open the heavy wooden door. It crashed against the wall with a loud thud, but she was unfazed by the sound of the bang or the rattling blinds on his little window leading out into the outer office. Tessa looked on as the brilliant sunlight poured in from the full paned windows lining the back walls of the office, giving the office a more spectacular atmosphere than the intimate dim lit darkness of night she had become so accustomed to. Right now, she did not have a care for whatever the setting, all she knew was that Bryson was there and that was the important thing.

Standing tall in front of his no longer ominous desk, he turned slowly around to face her. His form, tall, strong, and towering over her as she rushed forward to take him in her arms. The feel of his firm body against hers, lent itself to the realization that they fit perfectly together, and how right it was for her to be so close to him, just at this moment and forever.

Tessa held him closer to her still, and felt herself let out a sigh of relief as his strong arms soon enveloped her small frame, reciprocating her sentiments. He leaned forward and rested his head on the top of hers. She was right, they were a perfect fit, and they should never be parted again. Especially not for any foolishness like that of hers the previous night.

"I'm so, so sorry." Tessa finally said, pulling away just enough to look into his beautifully crafted face, with his precise cheek bones and firm freshly shaven jawline. "I don't know what came over me, I should have just allowed myself to trust you, but..." Her words were stopped short by the soft and lingering placement of a gentle kiss on her lips. She stood there in a state of stun and wonderment. Tessa knew that they were past the point where words were necessary for them to communicate their feelings to one another.

Tessa's body tingled with anticipation as she felt the firm caressing stroke of his able hands slide up her figure and to her neck; where his fingers were in her hair once again. Then, the soft, deep palms of his large, strong hands clasped her face as he continued to kiss her. He paused for a moment to gaze into her star filled green eyes, as she blinked at him like someone waking from a long sleep.

"You have nothing to be sorry for. I promise you Tessa that you have no reason not to trust me. No reason to doubt me, not now not ever." Bryson proclaimed to her in his tender, deep masculine voice that travelled into her ears and seemed to sing to her soul. She let out the sigh of someone who had finally found peace, someone who finally feels like they have truly arrived home.

Tessa leaned her body in closer to his as he continued to kiss her. She savored the taste of him on her tongue and the feel of his full lips on her face, as well as the slight scrape of his teeth on her jawline and chin. The surge of their collective passions roared with them, and Tessa could almost hear the primal beat of drums within her ears, to which she was not certain if there were actually drums or if it was the fervent pounding of her own heart.

She became aware of the open door behind them and desired it to be shut if things were going to go as far as she knew they were about to. Tessa raised a finger to Bryson's lips signaling him to stop for a moment. She smiled at him longingly as she began to turn for the door. Suddenly, the expression on his face changed from one of pleasure to one of bewilderment. This struck her with a wave of confusion until she turned to face the door completely and beheld the sight of a man of average height in a cheap suit. Tessa stopped dead in her tracks as the man began to make his advance into the room.

"Mr. Bryson Stafford," the man stated with an air of authority, and Tessa noticed the badge hanging from a laniard in front of his bright blue tie.

"Yes, that's me, what is this about?" Bryson asked a little stunned himself, as she was.

The man turned to a few others who stood in the outer office and motioned them to come in. He began to direct them to start taking the trays of files out of the filing cabinets. Tessa looked around, completely lost as to what was happening. She looked to Bryson for some kind of explanation, but knew she would not find the answer in him for he appeared to be just as lost as she.

"I am Detective Bullard, of the NYPD Fraud division, working in tandem with the Internal Revenue Service and the SEC. We received some crucial information that says your company has been embezzling funds from the payroll of its employees for quite some time now. How do you answer these charges?" The detective clarified.

"Um, the only thing I can say is that I don't really know what to say. I mean, how long did you say this was going on?" Bryson queried, taking his place beside Tessa.

"As far as we can tell from our information, this has been going on since the year 2008. So, nearly eleven years and a few months...give or take." The man informed him.

"Well, with all due respect, detective. If I may?" piped in Tessa, raising her hand to get his attention.

"Yes, ma'am, and what do you have to do with all of this?" The detective responded matter-of-factly.

"Well, Bryson...Mr. Stafford here, and I have been conducting a bit of an investigation of our own, when I discovered this myself a few weeks ago." Tessa explained to him, her eye line slightly diverted by the swarm of bodies rushing around the room and traipsing out with various boxes of files.

"Oh, you have, have you?" began the detective with a slightly comical look on his face. "With, Mr. Stafford? And, who are you, ma'am?"

"I am Tessa Clayton, I'm a first floor accounting analyst." Tessa replied.

"Ah, I see, he had you looking into this matter for him?" The detective had retrieved a small steno pad from the inner pocket of his sport coat and started to make notes in it.

"Yes, and I will be more than happy to furnish you and the rest of your colleagues with the information that we have accrued over the last few weeks. You see, we didn't want to just run to the authorities until we had something absolutely concrete." Tessa defended.

"Well, that is completely understandable. And yes, we will be happy with any and all information you can provide. So I am going to need you to come down to the station as well and make a statement." said the detective.

"Yes, of course, whatever you need." Tessa reassured him.

"Yes, we will all cooperate as much as we can." Bryson reassured him as well.

"That sounds a bit funny coming from you, Mr. Stafford. Almost as funny as the idea that you were investigating this problem yourself." The detective jabbed, pointing his pen in Bryson's direction with a bit of a smirk on his face.

"Well, I know we may not be the most capable of investigators. But we did with what we had." Bryson countered.

"That isn't what I mean, I just think it's funny that the guy who is at the root of this whole thing is 'conducting' an investigation into his own embezzlement scheme." explained the detective.

"I'm sure I don't know what you are talking about, detective." Bryson defended himself. Tessa saw that his firm jaw was beginning to clinch nervously. There was a hint of sincerity in his voice, but she could not be completely certain.

"Oh, so you don't know anything about your safety deposit box at TD Bank, with nearly a quarter of a million dollars in deposits over the last several months? You don't know anything about all of these payroll health and wellness deposit receipts with your signature on them for deviation of funds?" The detective pulled the file folder out from under his arm and opened it handing it to Bryson.

Bryson took a look at the open file in his hand with a dumb founded expression on his face. "Well, I do have an account with them, but..." Bryson couldn't finish his sentence before Tessa had nearly ripped the file from his grip and began to peruse it herself.

The more she looked, the more horrified she became. Everything seemed to add up as she ran over all of the calculations and diagrams from the last few weeks. This was the end to the trail of untraceable funds. No wonder she was having so much trouble finding it, it was because he was blinding her from finding the truth. Her passion for him was soon replaced with humiliation and rage. Rage at the fact that she had been so stupid to let her guard down and trust him. Once again, she had left herself open to be lied to and taken advantage of, like the sap she apparently was. She began to wonder if she had some kind of a sign on her forehead or target on her back that read, "Lie to me, I'm gullible."

Bryson had obviously seen the change of expression on her face because he took her arms firmly in his hands and turned her to face him. "Tessa, you have to listen to me. I can explain this, I can, somehow. I'm innocent, I promise you. I told you I wouldn't lie to you. You have to believe me." He pleaded desperately, his eyes seeming to shine even more with his fear and bewilderment. But she knew better than to believe it, at least she wanted to. She found herself being very conflicted, and her heart warred with her mind as she wanted so desperately to believe that what he was saying was true. But she just couldn't, her logic wouldn't allow it.

The detective pulled the hand cuffs from behind his back and moved forward to take Bryson's hands. "Mr. Stafford, I am placing you under arrest for the crime of fraud and embezzlement." he stated, as he placed Bryson's hands behind his back and fastened on the handcuffs. They snapped shut with a jarring click that seemed to bring Tessa further into her senses.

"I want to believe you Bryson but you see, the thing is. It's like I told you before, people lie. I understand this better than anyone because of how much they have lied to me and tried to sweep things under the rug. Why did I allow myself to think you would be any different? Especially after how you reacted when I first met you." Tessa said firmly, beginning to storm out of the office, leaving him to his fate.

"But, Tessa, you can't believe that of me. I've changed, I really have and all because of you." Bryson continued to plead, sadness filling his eyes and fear washing over the rest of his expression.

"No, you haven't changed. You only pretended to, and this is why I stick to the numbers, Bryson. Even though they may change, they never lie." Tessa punctuated her words by swiftly turning, and making her way through the bustling crowd of officials in blue wind breakers, with various acronyms of the different respective agencies

CHAPTER 11

Disclosures

———————— • ————————

Tessa sat on the well-worn thrift store couch in the apartment she shared with Shalena. They sipped wine while mindlessly watching a twilight zone marathon on TLC. She needed time to recover from what she felt was one of the worst shocks she had received in the last two years. And she had been through quite a bit, so that was really saying something.

Tessa sat there in silence mulling over the events of the last few days in her mind. How could she have been so stupid as to let her guard down, enough for someone to take advantage of her like that yet again? she thought, as she continued to mentally kick herself.

She held out her empty tumbler to Shalena for a much needed top up and she gladly obliged, nearly over filling Tessa's glass and giggling. "Well, it was almost out anyway, and to throw it out like that would just be alcohol abuse." Shalena laughed. "Ooo, I love this one!" she delightedly squealed in Tessa's ear, and Tessa turned to see that another episode had come on.

"What's this one about again?" Tessa asked, taking another sip of her Moscato.

"Oh you know, this is that doppelgänger shit. The one where that lady has another lady like steal her identity, and by the end you don't know if it's the real lady or her evil twin." Shalena explained.

"Oh, wow, that's pretty scary." Tessa remarked, snuggling herself closer to her friend and deeper into the cushions.

"Yeah, that shit is super scary. You know we had a girl that used to work at the bar who had her identity stolen. She almost got arrested, like the cops came to the bar and everything." Shalena told her.

"Oh my god. What happened?" Tessa asked, surprised.

"Well, they didn't take her in once we proved that she was in the hospital having a baby, at the time that the other lady did all of those things they were going to arrest her for." Shalena said.

"Well, that's good." Tessa responded, feeling the wheels already beginning to turn in her mind.

"Yeah, we just had to explain to them that there was no way she could be in two places at once. It's just common sense, you know?" As soon as Shalena got out the last word, a light went off in Tessa's mind. That was it, all of the numbers and dates on the receipts she had seen in the file, earlier that morning, came flooding back into her thoughts. She darted up from the couch and ran to her room to get her laptop.

Over the next couple of hours, she was completely consumed in going over all of the research she had accrued. It all made sense now, and she was more certain than she had ever been that she had the key to solving this mystery and catching the actual culprit.

Once Tessa was confident that she had she had gathered enough information, she leapt out from her apartment and made a call to her favorite cabbie to take her to the police station. She knew that she only just had enough to catch detective Bullard before he left for the night.

When she finally made it to the police station, she ran up the steps and stopped at the front desk. The woman sitting at the front desk looked up unenthused. "Can I help you, ma'am?"

"Um, yes, I am here to see detective Bullard about the Stafford Financial fraud case, I have some information for him." explained Tessa.

"Alright, just give me a moment." the woman informed her, as she picked up the receiver to the black phone on her desktop. "Detective Bullard, I have someone up here for you. They say they have information on your fraud case." The lady hung up the receiver. "He'll be out here in a moment ma'am, if you'll just wait right here."

Tessa waited only for a moment before she caught sight of the detective she had seen earlier in the day, coming out into the corridor and motioning for her to follow him into the back of the precinct. She followed his direction and made her way down the long hallway, past lock up and through the maze of desks, before finally arriving at his. He gestured for her to take a seat.

"Can I offer you anything? Coffee? I think we might have some tea, a water?" he asked hospitably.

"Oh, thank you, no. I'm alright." Tessa declined.

"So you said you have some information for me about the case?" asked the detective, taking a seat himself behind the desk.

"Yes," she began and retrieved the laptop from her bag. She placed it on his desk and turned it around to face him. Tessa watched as the middle aged gentleman put on his reading glasses, to get a better look of what she was trying to show him. "You see here, this is all of the information I have accrued about the embezzlement. There are names and time stamps on all of the documents."

"I see you were very thorough, miss Clayton." praised the detective.

"The reason I am showing you this is because when all of the time stamps of these documents were put in, Mr. Stafford, Bryson, was with me in his office going over this evidence. So he couldn't have been at the bank making those last deposits that were in the bottom of this file." She reached over and opened the file folder on his desk that she recognized from earlier. Tessa's finger made a slight scraping sound, as it slid down the matte printer paper to the appropriate section of the document. The detective leaned over to peer at the passages she pointed to.

"So what you're telling me is that someone else, made these deposits in his name and forged his signature." the detective responded.

"I'm telling you precisely that." Tessa proclaimed.

"And who are you saying would do such a thing?" The detective asked, leaning back in his chair.

Tessa returned to her seat. "His brother, Theo Stafford."

"That is a very plausible theory, go on." The detective rolled his hand.

"The reason I say this is because he has had his eye on becoming CEO for a long time now, and what would be more perfect than for him to become CEO to continue to cover his tracks." Tessa said.

"Well, from what I can see from all of the information that you have here, that is a pretty convincing theory. However, it is all circumstantial, and it probably won't stand up in court with just your word to back it up." The detective informed her.

"What if I could get him to confess to it on tape? Would that hold up in court?" Tessa proposed.

"Yeah, if you could do that. But there is no guarantee that you would be able to do that." said the detective.

"Oh, believe me. I can."

CHAPTER 12

Sheets of Balance

———— • ————

Tessa showed up very late to the office and strategically made her way to the back elevator, which quickly took her up to the top floor of the building. She was on an entirely new mission now, and that was to save Bryson. She felt bad now for a completely different reason than she had before. She was remorseful for the fact that she had allowed her own past hurt to cloud her judgment, and cause her to not believe him when he was actually being honest with her. This was something else that she was going to have to work on about herself. But she couldn't worry about that right now. She had to focus on getting Theo to confess.

Tessa briskly marched down the hallway until she came to the open door of his office. She adjusted her breasts and prepared for what it might take to get him to give her the goods. Lingering in the door way, she waited for him to notice that someone was standing behind him.

He turned slightly and threw a glance over his shoulder, signifying his sensing of someone else's presence. "Oh, hello, Tessa. What a pleasant surprise. What are you doing here so late?" He greeted her with a flash of what she once thought was his charming smile. It now came off as cheesy and insincere.

"I just came back to get my things, noticed that the door was open and wondered who was in here so late. Burning the midnight oil?" she responded, coming further into the opening of the room.

"Well, someone has to, now that our fearless leader is in jail, and the other has taken to his sick bed." Theo answered.

"Yeah, that's really too bad how that all turned out. That's why I'm leaving for good now." Tessa said.

"I can only imagine how bad of a taste this whole experience has left in your mouth." Theo stated.

Tessa moved in closer and sat against the front of the desk, looking down with the best downtrodden expression she could muster. Theo leaned closer to her and lifted up her face to look into her eyes. "He really broke your heart didn't he? That bastard."

"Yeah, I just can't help but feel guilty for allowing him to take advantage of me that way, you know? Who would have thought he was capable of doing something like this?" Tessa whimpered a little.

"I know, it's really a shame what you find out about people. Especially your own family." said Theo.

"I guess that is why he was considered the cleverer one out of the two of you, because he was able to run this scheme for so long without getting caught." Tessa prodded.

Theo chuckled and raised an eyebrow. "Ha, but you see it is not the clever ones that get caught. It's the ones that are stupid." He countered.

"Oh really, what do you mean?" Tessa began to feel like she was beginning to make head way.

"What I mean, my dear lady, is that he is not the cleverer one of us two, because he got caught." Theo clarified.

"So are you saying you were involved with this too?" Tessa asked, seeming amazed.

"Oh darling, I'm not just involved. I'm the fucking mastermind!" He exclaimed throwing up his arms.

"So what are you saying?" she asked again.

"I'm saying that all of this was me, I am the one who set up the deposit box in his name and saved the whole scheme with a failsafe, so that when shit finally hit the fan, it would all come crashing down on him. And we would be left in the clear." Theo explained.

"We?" She looked at him quizzically.

"Yes, my father. But he won't be around that much longer. So that just leaves me with everything. But I don't really mind that." stated Theo. "You see, that is why it would be such a bad time for you to leave. I could really use someone with your skill set at my side right about now. Imagine all of the money you could make, we would have the lion's share, and perhaps more if you were interested." He sat on the edge of the desk beside her, and inched in closer, nudging against her arm.

Tessa stood from her position and began to skew her way to the door." I appreciate the job offer, but I think I'm just going to take a break for a little while. Maybe go into something a little more small time. This is all too big for me."

"I understand, just know that if you ever need me you'll know where to find me." Theo called after her.

"Oh believe me I will." she replied and continued to walk out, when suddenly, Bryson came bursting into the door way. Before Theo could say anything, he had descended upon him and began punching him in the face. The rushing fury of bodies in a tussle began to fly about the room, creating a terrible destructive ruckus as they fought. Tessa stood there unsure of what to do, until the squad of police detectives that had been waiting down the hall, burst in and broke up the fight.

It did not take them very long to slap the cuffs on Theo and begin to rush him out of the room, kicking and screaming expletives at everyone.

Bryson quickly ran over to Tessa and scooped her up in his tight embrace. She fell into him, and began to cry for joy and relief as well as remorse for how she had behaved.

"I love you, Tessa. And I'm so sorry for giving you any reason to doubt me." Bryson whispered into her delicately formed ear.

"I know, and I'm sorry for not having the faith in you I should have." Tessa apologized as she gently stroked his hair.

Bryson pulled away slightly and gazed deeply into her eyes, making sure that she fully understood what he was about to say. "There is no reason for you to apologize. Just be glad this is all over now, and we can move forward from here." He embraced her once again.

Tessa felt the tap of a firm hand on her arm and she opened her eyes to find the detective standing there. "Ahem," he announced himself.

Tessa and Bryson pulled away from each other and faced him. She quickly wiped the tears from her eyes and pulled the recording device and wire from inside of her jacket. "Did you get everything you needed?" she asked.

"Oh, yes, more than enough, and it's going to put him away for a long time." the detective answered. "Good work, both of you." he patted Bryson on the arm as he began to walk away. Turning to Bryson once more before his final departure, he said to Bryson, "Mr. Stafford, if I were you, I would hold on to this one. She's a keeper."

C H A P T E R 13

Closing Statements

————— • —————

Bryson sat in the dreary gray interrogation room, across the well-worn, scratched up aluminum table from his father. Thinking back to his younger days where he spent a lot of the time in places like this, at least until his father came to bail him out, he wondered for a moment if all police stations had some kind of a wholesale option for furniture like this all over the country. Now the tables had officially turned, and he was facing his father who was on the other side of the law.

"I feel a little strange asking you this, but what do you have to say for yourself? What the fuck were you thinking, Dad, you of all people...embezzlement? You were the one that always told us the only good money is honest money." Bryson scolded his father with a heartbroken and faithless laden tone in his voice.

"I know, son. This is certainly not an easy pill to swallow. It certainly wasn't for me when this whole thing began. But you have to understand the situation I was in. I was truly a man caught between a rock and a hard place." his father replied solemnly, toying with the ring of their family crest on his middle finger.

Bryson had never seen his father look as he did now. He appeared to him as a tired and old man who had truly been run over by life. He had never looked as much like an old man as he did now.

"What happened? Help me understand, father." Bryson pleaded, leaning forward.

"You know how they say that necessity is the mother of invention. But what they don't tell you is that he is also the father of crime. The ultimate flip side of the coin that I wish I had never had the occasion to visit or see. When the bubble burst so suddenly in 2008, we were left holding the bag for a lot of people. Everyone around us was crumbling one by one, having to down size, laying off employees by the droves, and many of them having no other recourse but to close their doors altogether. It was only a matter of time before we were to be next on the chopping block. So we were left with no other option but to concoct some sort of plan to save us, to save everyone. Especially if there was going to be anything left for your brother to carry on the family name, and provide for your families whenever you ventured to have any. So, against my better judgement, we devised a plan to create a couple of shell companies where we could funnel money that would just be run back into the coffers of the company. This way we could tell all the necessary people that we were still able to keep everyone we had on staff, because we were making more than enough profit to pay our people. So those contractors for the memorial hospital and other things like that were not actually people. It seemed wise to me because I was being told we were not hurting anyone. It was truly a victimless crime." His father finished confessing. "I'm sorry son." he added, after seeing the expression on Bryson's face that he took for shame. "This is why I didn't tell you, because I knew that you would be ashamed of me. And that, is worse than any impending jail sentence. Or death sentence rather. For you know I won't make it outside of six months. My health won't allow it." Abram coughed violently, hacking up blood into his handkerchief.

"I don't think they'll let you die in here. No jury in the state would sentence you to die in prison. Especially, once they understand your motives. I just don't understand why you didn't come to me, father. I could have helped you stop." Bryson said.

"Don't you think I tried to stop, many times. It was just so difficult once we had gotten started. It just snowballed into a monster I could no longer control. Particularly after your brother got involved. We were fools to think there would be a way to stop it once we got started, without hurting someone anyway." His father responded.

"That's alright father, you don't have to explain yourself to me any further. I understand and I don't blame you for anything." He moved to the other side of the table and placed a kiss on his father's forehead. "You know, dad, I was always afraid that you would think that I was too weak to live up to your standards, and incapable of taking the reins of your company, after everything that I have done to disappoint you." projected Bryson.

"Oh, my son. You never had any reason to be afraid of that. Every man must take the time in his life to sow his wild oats. I am just glad that I was able to give you enough of the life you deserved, to be able to enjoy it while you could." His father smiled up at him, taking his hand firmly in his. Bryson smiled down at his father, feeling a swell of affection he had never known from his father before. He began to get up from the edge of the table and depart the room, when his father pulled at his hand once more. "I just want you to know, son, I see that you have turned out to be a far better and more honorable man than I. And, I see you as completely capable of not only preserving my legacy, but making it better than it ever was. For this, sir, you have truly earned my respect." He squeezed his hand to drive his point home.

A feeling of pride and love for his father grew within his chest as he knelt down to embrace the old man. Bryson finally knew that he had achieved the ultimate goal of his life. The love and respect of his father, and the knowledge that if he were to never see him again, he would be alright with that, because he knew now how he truly felt about him.

Bryson walked out of the police station. The glare of the mid afternoon sun hitting him square in the face, making him have to use his hand like a visor to clear his vision. His eyes scanned the street, and finally landed on the sight of his black, convertible mustang, with a beautiful dark haired lady sitting in the front passenger seat. This filled his heart with a slight giddiness, and he knew that the day that lay before him was going to be a great one. Rather, the life that lay before him was going to be a spectacular one. He walked with a new bounce in his step, down the steps and across the side walk to the car. Placing his hands on the door, he leaned in and placed a fervent kiss on her awaiting and welcoming lips.

Savoring the fact that they now belonged to him, as did the rest of her. Especially her heart.

"Are you alright, my love?" asked Tessa, stroking his cheek caringly.

Bryson looked down and kissed her lingering palm. "Yeah, I got what I wanted I suppose. Just not the way that I would have liked it. Not the way I would have imagined it even." he said.

"I know, honey, I'm sorry." She did her best to console him. "You have to take the good with the bad, I guess." she added.

"We don't always get things the way we want them." he grumbled, scuffing his feet on the pavement below.

"No, but whatever life hands to us now, we will be here to face it with each other. And, there is no one else whose side I would rather be at." Tessa assured him.

With these words of encouragement, Bryson picked up his chin and began to make his way to the driver's side of the car. The bounce had returned to his step, and he hopped in without even opening the door. Tessa let out a hearty squeal and a laugh that he had never heard from her before. This was something that he knew he could definitely get used to. Things like the beautiful light colored sundress that she wore now, as opposed to the harsh grays and blues of the business clothes he was so accustomed to seeing her in. She finally looked happy and fulfilled, as happy and fulfilled as he felt when he was with her.

"I would like to thank you for choosing to fly with Bryson airlines. Please fasten your seat belts and keep your chair backs and tray tables in their locked and upright positions." He quipped, leaning in her direction. He playfully kissed her as she clasped his face with a giggle. As she pulled away, she let out a sigh of satisfaction, and asked, "Where to, El Capitan?"

"Let's just see where the road takes us, shall we." he replied as he started the engine, and Tessa raised her arms and let out a shout that made him smile.

They pulled away from the cut and drove down the surprisingly nearly empty street. Driving swiftly in the direction of the bright, mid-day sun, happy in the knowledge that wherever the road of life would lead them, they would be there to face it together.

TOC